"Would you mind fixing a fresh pot of coffee?"

His voice was deep, gentle, out of keeping with his rough, tough looks. "I'm going to be making a midnight check on that heifer," he explained.

"All right." She turned back to the ranch house, and he fell into step beside her. The moon was an alchemist, she thought, gilding his sun-streaked hair and turning the gray to silver.

He caught her staring. "What's on your mind?"

"Just thinking about the moonlight," she hedged. "About how people sometimes say it's as bright as day. But I don't think so. It's a soft, caressing light, not a merciless, revealing one."

"I didn't think you were the kind to find beauty in nature."

"You don't know anything about me!" she retorted.

The look in his eyes made her nervous as he said quietly, "Then tell me."

Dear Reader,

Welcome to summer, and welcome to another fine month of reading from Silhouette Intimate Moments. We have some exciting books in store for you, not just this month, but all summer long. Let me start with our June titles, then give you a peek at what's coming up in the future.

First, there's *That McKenna Woman*, the first book in Parris Afton Bonds' Mescalero Trilogy. Parris used her home state of New Mexico as the location of the Mescalero Cattle Company, then peopled the ranch with some of the most charismatic characters you'll ever find. Tom Malcolm and Marianna McKenna couldn't be less alike, but that doesn't stop them from discovering a love as big as the West. And the family created by their marriage provides the basis for the other two books in the series, books we know you'll look forward to reading.

Another special book for June is Kathleen Eagle's *More Than a Miracle*, a follow-up to *Candles in the Night* (Silhouette Special Edition #437). This is the story of a woman who, forced to give up her child, now embarks on a desperate mission to find her son. Her only help comes from the man they call McQuade, and even then, it may take more than a miracle to make her dream come true.

During the rest of the summer, look for books by old favorites like Lucy Hamilton (whose Dodd Memorial Hospital Trilogy ends in July with *Heartbeats*), Heather Graham Pozzessere and Emilie Richards. They're just a few of the writers whose work will be waiting for you— only in the pages of Silhouette Intimate Moments.

Sincerely,

Leslie J. Wainger
Senior Editor, Silhouette Books

Parris Afton Bonds

That McKenna Woman

Silhouette Intimate Moments

Published by Silhouette Books New York

America's Publisher of Contemporary Romance

SILHOUETTE BOOKS
300 East 42nd St., New York, N.Y. 10017

ISBN: 0-373-07241-4

First Silhouette Books printing June 1988

Printed in the U.S.A.

PARRIS AFTON BONDS

has been writing since she was six, though she didn't turn professional until her family moved to Mexico. She gives the credit for her several literary awards to her husband and sons, who have given unstintingly of their love and support.

For Peggy Curtis,
who gamely braved the research trip

Chapter 1

Cell block B's cubicles were small, each one furnished with a bed, a sink and a toilet. For the last two hours, since returning at seven o'clock from breakfast in the mess hall, she had prowled her cell. Prowled dangerously close to the outer limits of her sanity. Nervous perspiration dotted her temples, upper lip and palms. The drip of the faucet punctuated each glacially slow minute. Come nine o'clock, she would be a free woman.

Well, that had to be qualified, she reflected grimly. She would be free from incarceration behind locked door after locked door, imprisoned so deep in the bowels of the maximum-security prison that the chance glimpses of precious daylight blinded her.

"Freedom," she had come to learn during the past five days, was not an absolute term. There were variations on freedom. For the next six months, her freedom, according to the district judge in El Paso, would be defined as doing service duty with the Mescalero Cattle Company. That was a much better fate than serving a full seven years behind bars, seeing her nine-year-old daughter solely on visitation days.

Because she had good references, was a first-time offender and a prominent figure, and—most of all— because she had insisted on her innocence throughout the entire three-month ordeal, the federal parole officer's recommendation had been accepted. The sentence of seven years had been suspended, and she had been put on comprehensive probation for three years, the first six months of which would constitute labor under the new service duty program.

As the judge had put it, "If you're going to play hard, Miss McKenna, you're going to work hard."

Marianna was jerked out of her reverie by the sound of a voice.

"Get your gear, honey," Chloe warned. "The Queen's coming for you."

Chloe, Marianna's black cellmate, jerked her head toward the corridor. Somehow the inmates who had served lengthy sentences acquired a kind of telepathy in relation to the penitentiary's inner activities. Long before anything happened, the long-term prisoners knew of its impending occurrence.

Marianna froze beside the bars. Yes, she thought. If she listened carefully, she could hear approaching footsteps, accompanied by strident female voices filled with curiosity, animosity and desperation.

She whirled back to her side of the cell and began stuffing her few belongings, mostly toiletries, into the duffel bag provided by the prison. The cell wasn't endowed with a mirror, but she wouldn't have bothered to check her appearance anyway. Without makeup, her grooming had been reduced to the basics. Her usually thick, flyaway red hair was almost lank now and restrained by an elastic band at her nape. The shapeless olive-green dress she wore made her look like a drab housewife of the thirties.

The photographers for the major dailies would have a field day this morning.

A sharp buzz from the electronic control panel activated the opening of the barred door. Its clanging bolts echoed in the vast correctional facility. The Queen stood on the other side. Accompanying the middle-aged prison matron were two other guards, their hands resting lightly on their hips. All three women wore khaki shirts and slacks.

The Queen smiled, a smile that made Marianna shudder more than once. To be a prison guard required only a high school diploma or its equivalent, but the matron's features indicated keen intelligence, albeit a cruel, feral one. The hefty woman controlled all that went on in cell block B. The tough leaders of the various prison gangs paid her tribute in the form of bribes. After her introduction to the woman, Marianna had begun to suspect that anything more than a few days in cell block B would mean attracting unwanted attention from the matron.

"Get your butt moving, glitter girl," the Queen said now. "The warden's ready to see you."

Chloe gave Marianna a thumbs-up sign. Marianna managed a smile, then stepped forward.

"Not so fast," the Queen said. She nodded curtly, and one of the guards produced a pair of handcuffs. The prison operated according to such archaic rules that even the possibility of being shackled at the waist and ankles was not preposterous.

"I'm leaving this morning," Marianna said. "Is this necessary?"

"You can always stay, glitter girl."

The Queen's suggestive grin cut short any further protest. Marianna extended her wrists. The metal was cold, the clamps tight. One more reminder of her captivity. One more nightmare.

As Marianna, flanked by the two female guards, followed the Queen down the corridor, catcalls and taunts erupted from the other female inmates. Marianna shivered. She couldn't get out of this hellhole soon enough. The first thing she wanted was a bath.

Yet there was still the discharge center to go through, the mandatory mug shot and fingerprinting before release, even though she had submitted to the same procedure upon arrival. "A matter of procedure," the clerk told her without even looking up from the film pack she was sliding into the camera. This latest mode of humiliation—posing for frontal and profile shots—was slight in comparison to the five days and four nights she had spent in cell block B.

At last the processing was over, and Marianna, still handcuffed, was escorted along the catwalk to the warden's office. The spacious, well-appointed room afforded her the first breath of comfort she had experienced in five days. At first she blinked at the dazzling sunlight, which hurt her eyes. Then her eyes began to focus. The sight of the potted ivy, soaking up March's fleeting sunshine on the sill of a bay window, was her undoing. Weakness, the kind that made her want to cry, welled up in her. She steeled herself, straightened her shoulders and lifted her chin.

The warden, an impeccably dressed man with silvering hair and horn-rimmed glasses, looked up from an open file folder on his desk. "Miss McKenna, please be seated. I've only got a few more forms to sign, and then your release to the Mescalero Cattle Company will be finalized."

She seated herself in the tufted leather chair near the desk. She sat with her spine straight, a habit left over from her days at a Catholic school on Guam. The school had been ruled by a despotic nun, and along with an excellent command of Latin, Marianna had acquired self-discipline. Unable to place her shackled hands on the armrests, she left them clasped in her lap. As the warden began scribbling his signature on the forms, the room's unnerving silence began to bother her.

Soon, soon, she thought, I'll see Shyloh again. At least she wasn't taken from me!

Finished, the warden fixed her with a stern gaze. "I hope you have profited from your brief internment here, Miss McKenna. Trafficking in heroin is not fun and games. The hard manual labor you will be assigned over the next six months should convince you of that. I trust you will find yourself a sadder but wiser woman.''

Sadder but wiser. Older but wiser. Why was wiser always coupled with something unpleasant? ''When may I see my daughter, Warden?''

''She's waiting in the administration office, Miss McKenna. I'll remind you that any violation of your service duty will result in your daughter being placed in a children's home and your being sentenced to the full seven years in the penitentiary without parole.''

Even here she felt claustrophobic. Please get on with this! she pleaded silently. Set me free!

She swallowed. ''I understand.''

''Excellent. Then let me introduce you to Mr. Malcolm, into whose custody you are being placed.''

Marianna, following the direction of the warden's gaze, glanced over her left shoulder. She had been unaware that there was anyone else in the room. Behind her, in the corner, loomed a man, his shadow distorted by the walls to gigantic proportions. But when he uncoiled himself from the chair and stepped forward into the light, his massive size seemed only slightly diminished. He was all hard muscle and solid bone.

Her glance took in well-worn boots, faded jeans, a sheepskin jacket and a black Stetson clasped lightly in a large, weather-tanned hand. She felt compelled to stare into the mirrored sunglasses that hid his eyes, though she was sure he was making a full examination of her.

"Tom, this is Marianna McKenna. Miss McKenna, Tom Malcolm, of the Mescalero Cattle Company."

Automatically Marianna extended her hand, only to be reminded by the jangling handcuffs of her ignominious position. Her hands dropped awkwardly back into her lap. Attempting to maintain some semblance of dignity, she said, "I'm pleased to meet you, Mr—"

"A woman and child?" Tom Malcolm dismissed her with a grimace of his hard mouth. His jaw set, he focused his impatience on the warden. "Is the government run by a bunch of wackos?"

The warden passed her file to the man. "It's a first for the Feds, Tom, and no doubt a last, too."

Mortified, Marianna dropped her gaze to her clenched hands and their bracelets of steel.

Tom slapped the folder against his thigh. "A dealer, huh?"

Her head snapped up. "That's not true!"

She could feel his eyes measuring her behind the opaque sunglasses. He looked to be well into his late thirties. His nose was crooked, as if it had been broken several times. His hair, badly in need of a haircut, was his only apparent attractive quality; it was a thick, dark brown that glinted both with sun streaks and the telltale smoke-gray of age, an unusual combination.

"You've been convicted," he said, his voice deep. "The law says you're guilty, and you'll have to convince me otherwise."

Her teeth clenched. Would she have to go through the rest of her life proving her innocence?

He ignored the withering glare she shot him and turned back to the warden. "Take her handcuffs off before we leave your office. No need for her daughter to see them."

She hadn't cried once during the three-month ordeal. Maybe it was pride that had prevented her. But for the second time in the space of half an hour she was moved nearly to tears—this time by the rancher's act, which she somehow sensed was uncharacteristically considerate.

She blinked back angry tears. Damn it, she didn't owe this man any gratitude. If not for people like him, ready to believe the worst about her, she wouldn't have been reduced to these circumstances—her career ruined, her finances decimated, her life and Shyloh's in shreds. She and her daughter should have remained in the Hollywood Hills instead of moving last year to Mesilla.

The sleepy little village outside Las Cruces, New Mexico, had seemed a perfect place to settle. The cost of living was low, enabling her to hire local live-in care for Shyloh when she herself had to be on location. But the town was still close enough to El Paso's international airport, only forty-five minutes away, to make travel to various film locations easier for her.

Ironically, Marianna had wanted to escape Tinsel Town's fast life, to make a stable, homey environment for her painfully shy daughter, the kind of life she herself had never known in all her thirty-four years. Precisely because of her rootless past, she had chosen to slow her acting career, which had brought her accolades for her sensitive portrayals of a wide variety of characters. She had given up several juicy roles in order to spend more time with Shyloh.

Despite her blurred vision, she saw Tom Malcolm hunker down before her to free her from her bondage. The handcuffs fell away, and her hands—soft, chilled—lay palm up, a symbol of surrender, in his much larger ones, warm and callused. He seemed as bemused as she by the counterpoint.

"They won't stay this way," he mused in a deep voice, a voice as deep as she imagined God's would be. But then, he would be playing God as far as her life was concerned, wouldn't he?

She forced her gaze to meet his scrutiny unflinchingly, but she encountered only the impenetrable silver glare of his reflective sunglasses. Whatever compassion his action had led her to expect was contradicted by his mouth: flat and unyielding, and with a dangerous crease at one end warning her that he didn't comply with the social niceties adhered to by her coterie of friends and business associates.

"Come along," he ground out, rising smoothly to his full height. "The day's not getting any shorter."

It took her little more than ten minutes to change into the salmon silk suit she had worn on entering the

penitentiary. Prison shampoo had left her hair looking dry and brittle, and a brush did little to restore its
vitality, so it was back to the rubber band. Fortu-
nately, years of film experience had taught her to artfully apply makeup in a minimum of time. When she
left the dressing room to meet Shyloh, the flickering
ember of her self-esteem was heating to a small but
warm glow. If only Tom Malcolm wouldn't douse it in
front of her daughter.

He was almost completely silent during the first few
minutes of their reunion, speaking only to suggest that
they begin the trip to the ranch, since time was passing and they had a long way to go.

Outside the administration building, the winter
wind whistled around her and Shyloh, who was
warmly dressed in a corduroy jumpsuit and jacket.
The morning cloud buildup hovered over the Frank-
lin Mountains, the ragged tail end of the Rockies.
Marianna hoped the weather wasn't an omen of their
immediate future.

Shyloh clung to her arm and warily eyed the score
of reporters waiting to pounce outside the prison gate.
Marianna was immediately barraged with shouted
questions. Automatic flashes were everywhere, blinding her. She had thought the paparazzi at the Cannes
Film Festival were disorderly, but this was chaos. Her
newest jailer took her arm and shouldered a path
through the press of newspeople for her and the be-
wildered Shyloh.

For years now, Marianna had managed to maintain a low profile, with her public relations firm dis-

pensing teasers to the media several times a month, just to make certain her name was kept before the public. This, however, was something she wanted kept private, if for no other reason than to protect her daughter. It was impossible, of course; one of Shyloh's schoolmates had already taunted her about her mother's arrest and trial. In simple but forthright terms, Marianna had told her daughter the truth, but that still hadn't prepared Shyloh for the pandemonium erupting around them now.

Despite their eagerness for the story, the newspapermen parted for Tom Malcolm's big frame, and he ushered her and Shyloh toward a cowboy rig, a black-and-tan four-wheel-drive pickup pulling a small stock trailer. Once inside the pickup, which was mud-splattered and stenciled with the words Mescalero Cattle Company, Marianna exhaled wearily.

Shyloh, sitting between Tom and her, kept glancing back at the horde of reporters. "Do you like being famous, Mom?"

Marianna couldn't keep her hands off the precious person she had come so close to losing. She smoothed her daughter's mop of hair, which was as unruly as her own but blond, like her former husband's. "Not particularly, pumpkin."

"I don't think I ever want to be famous, Mom."

Marianna managed a smile. "You don't have to if you don't want to. When you grow up, you can do anything you want."

"I want to be an artist," she announced. Last year it had been a nurse. She turned to the man and asked shyly, "Is that a cow you're pulling?"

"A steer."

"How do you tell the difference?"

The bracket at one end of his mouth deepened in amusement. "You'll learn how. You'll learn a lot about cattle over the next six months."

Marianna frowned at the man. She had wanted to be the one to prepare her daughter for this latest up-heaval in their lives. Now she spoke up quickly. "We're going to live at the Mescalero Cattle Ranch, babe. I'll be working there."

"Gee, that's great, Mom. We'll be together all the time now."

Guilt attacked Marianna, the kind that she sup-posed every working mother experienced, except that her work had required her absence for weeks, some-times months, at a time. When Shyloh had been a toddler, Marianna had taken her on location with her. But once Shyloh had started school, Marianna had had to make compromises between her roles as mother and actress. She knew she would be farther along in her career if she weren't a mother, but that would have been an awfully lonely path.

Relieved that Tom Malcolm wasn't predisposed to loquaciousness, she rested her head on the back of the seat and closed her eyes. For the past four nights she hadn't really slept, frightened by the howls she had heard from the other cells, howls the Queen and her contingent had either instigated or ignored.

Behind her lids, Marianna saw the vicious expressions, the leering ones, the sly ones, of the prisoners who had taunted her upon learning she was *that* Marianna McKenna. Then the cell itself took the place of the faces, its living walls inching in on her.

Her eyes snapped open. She could have used a cigarette, but her pack was in the duffel bag that Tom Malcolm had tossed in the back alongside feed sacks and blocks of salt. At her side, Shyloh was beginning to nod with drowsiness.

"Mr. Malcolm," Marianna said quietly, so as not to disturb her daughter, "I'd like to thank you for what you did back there—removing the handcuffs before Shyloh joined me."

"Hell, darlin', don't mistake that for a charitable act." He tugged the Stetson's curled brim lower. "I want both you and your daughter's willing cooperation at Mescalero. It's like breaking a bronc—brute force doesn't achieve anything. But if it takes brute force, I'm more than willing to accommodate."

"Delightful," she murmured. This man with power over her life and death had a dark sense of humor.

She would dearly have liked to see his eyes. The sunglasses kept her at an impersonal distance, making it difficult to read the man and adjust her actions accordingly. She had worked with wranglers on location, so she was familiar with the breed. They had to be able to shift for themselves and endure isolation. They seemed to thrive on physical hardship and a certain amount of danger. She supposed it was in their bones and blood.

The trophy belt buckle this man wore had obviously been won in some kind of rodeo. It was the equivalent of a military medal, she imagined. The cowboy had proven himself under fire. The buckle marked him as an expert in the skills the others of his kind most admired.

The way those sunglasses scanned the horizon, the way those even white teeth chewed his thin, unlighted cigar, told her that he thought she was an absurd irritant, an intrusion into his own steady existence, an annoyance that would require repair. "While your daughter's asleep," he rumbled, "is as good a time as any to discuss the rules you'll abide by while living at Mescalero."

Her mouth compressed into an obdurate line. She stared out the window at adobe homes banked by denuded cottonwoods. "I can hardly wait."

He ignored her sarcasm and went on talking in the whiskey-rough baritone she had first heard in the warden's office. "The conditions of your service duty are easy enough. You don't leave the ranch without one of the owners—either my sister or myself—accompanying you. You don't mess with firearms, and you don't mess around with the men."

Her head whipped toward him. "Mess with the men? Mr. Malcolm, I assure you, that is the farthest thing from my mind. I might demand that I be accorded the same right—that no men 'mess' with me!"

"Listen, darlin'," he said with elaborate politeness, "you no longer have any rights—least of all the right to make demands."

Feeling unable to carry the argument further with her daughter asleep between them, she retreated into silence. She broke it only to give him directions to her home.

He turned off Interstate 10 west of Las Cruces at the exit marked Mesilla. The village had been founded when Las Cruces had become a part of the United States after the war with Mexico in 1848 and some of its inhabitants had desired to remain citizens of Mexico. They had started a new settlement across the Rio Grande from Las Cruces and called it Mesilla. But after the Gadsden Purchase in 1854, Mesilla had wound up in the United States after all.

The potholed road that led to Mesilla had to date back to the Gadsden Purchase, Marianna thought darkly. But the jarring ride didn't seem to bother Shyloh, whose coltish legs were curled up under her slight body. The child slept happily in the nest created by Marianna's encircling arm.

Marianna had been so terrified that Shyloh would be taken from her that a silent litany of thanks ran repeatedly through her mind. Thank you, Lord. Thank you, Lord. Thank you!

As a child Marianna had attended church with her parents on a convenience basis. As an adult she attended in the same haphazard manner and figured she owed no one an explanation, since God seemed to know and understand her very well. But what had been in God's mind for the last three months she would dearly like to know.

"At the plaza, turn left," she said curtly.

Her house was a meandering ocher-colored adobe
set on two acres that backed up to the unpredictable
Rio Grande. The Mexican woman who kept house and
cared for Shyloh, a naturalized American citizen, met
her at the door. "*Señora*, I've been so worried! A
woman police officer, she came for Shyloh this morning. She told me all would be well, but I didn't know
what—"

"It's all right, Enriqueta. I have Shyloh. She's
asleep in the pickup."

"And you, *señora*? You are all right?" Enriqueta
was against government agents of any kind, particularly the border patrol, and she had been incensed
when she had learned her employer was going to jail.

Touched by the fifty-year-old woman's genuine
concern, Marianna patted her plump arm. "I'm fine,
Enriqueta. For the next six months, though, Shyloh
and I will be in the custody of—uh, staying with,
this...this man."

She glowered over her shoulder at Tom Malcolm,
who was lounging just inside the doorway, hat in one
hand, sunglasses in the other. Her glower faded at the
sight of his powerful features. His compelling eyes a
perennial squint from facing the harsh high-desert
elements. Their hazel color seemed uncommonly light
in contrast to his sun-toasted skin and dark brown
hair.

He grinned. A wolfish grin, she thought, noticing
the way his lip drew up at one end and his eyes narrowed. He unnerved her. He wasn't anything like the
plastic-handsome actors she worked with. This man

looked tough—and unable to appreciate anything better than a prizewinning heifer.

She felt his eyes on her as she and Enriqueta moved around the house, quickly packing the essentials Shyloh and she would need for the next six months. If she felt uneasy under Tom Malcolm's relentless regard in her own house, she thought, how much worse would it be in his?

After she and Enriqueta finished packing, she instructed the Mexican woman to forward all telephone messages and mail to her agent in Hollywood. "Trent will know how to reach me."

At the door, she paused beside her two suitcases and glanced expectantly at Tom Malcolm.

"You've got two hands, Miss McKenna. You'd better learn to use them."

He was right, of course. She could no longer expect doors to be opened for her and chairs to be pulled out. She flushed with embarrassment. That was the worst thing about being a redhead. Her emotional responses showed in a blaze across her cheeks. She arched one brow, an old defensive trick. "You don't like women, do you, Mr. Malcolm?"

"I don't like drug dealers."

This time she didn't even bother to protest her innocence. It didn't matter what he thought anyway, did it? What mattered was getting through the next six months. She picked up the heavy suitcases and followed him out the door.

The paved portion of the road to Mescalero followed the route of El Camino Real, the ancient road between Mexico City and Santa Fe. Foot soldiers, colonists, priests, conquistadores and caravans of ox carts had all traveled this trail. After a tauntly silent hour, Tom turned off onto a caliche road that paralleled the Mexican border some twenty miles away and rumbled over a cattle guard.

Shyloh awoke just as the pickup was passing between crumbling limestone walls that supported an arched iron grill announcing the Mescalero Cattle Company. "Are we there?" she asked, excitement brightening her pale cheeks.

"Not for another seventeen miles," Tom told her with that wolfish grin.

Shyloh didn't seem at all bothered by what masqueraded as his smile. "Gosh, Mescalero must be big! Bigger than Universal Studios."

The pickup crossed a considerable stretch of isolated country. After some thought, Marianna decided that "stretch" was an inappropriate description. The desert landscape wrinkled, folded and twisted into gulches, hogbacks, peaks, sand dunes and mesas. Yucca, juniper and greasewood were the only apparent vegetation.

At last she saw the towering tip of a windmill. Then scattered outbuildings came into view. Next she saw ocotillo-staked corrals, then an immense barn, what looked like a carriage house converted into a machine shed, adobe bunkhouses and an arena—with a grandstand, no less. In a more substantial corral made of creosote-dipped posts, a cowboy with a turkey feather in his hat was working cattle from the back of a mule.

Then the pickup reached the main house, which was surrounded by a low, mud brick wall and shaded by a few large mesquite and honey locust trees. The two-story house was built in the old Territorial style of soft rose adobe and roofed with corrugated iron, now rusted a deep reddish brown. Old-fashioned *canales*, or waterspouts, protruded from the flat roof. The hacienda was surrounded by elaborate wooden verandas on both levels. "Impressive" was the word that came to Marianna's mind. It was impressive and solid. A sense of antiquity pervaded the place.

On closer inspection, however, she could see that Mescalero was in a state of deterioration. Fences needed mending, the barn painting; the yard wall—along with what appeared to be a gristmill—was crumbling. The lower veranda was weathered, and warped in places where the cedar bushes teased the balustrade.

Tom Malcolm halted the pickup alongside a Jeep and several other four-wheelers parked outside the yard, then propped his forearms on the steering wheel, staring glumly outside. A stiff wind took dust from the scrubland and sent it swirling up through the dry trees. The clouds hurried to the western mountains, as if they were being sucked over the horizon.

"Welcome to Mescalero," he said, his voice echoing the harsh reality of her new home.

He swung down out of the cab. His long, ambling stride easily covered the windswept sand as he passed through a weathered gate. A dog that looked part coyote padded after him, and an owl, perched in a bare tree, ruffled its feathers at the man's approach.

Marianna watched until he reached the shadowed veranda and was out of sight—this man who for the next six months owned her, body and soul.

Chapter 2

I don't reckon you're gonna be any help, but I'd be obliged if you didn't hinder me, either."

Tom's sister, almost as tall as he and whipcord-lean, looked Marianna up and down, her lips pressed tightly together. Marianna judged the woman to be young, not more than twenty-one or so. At the sight of Shyloh, peeking out from behind Marianna, Roberta's expression eased somewhat, but not enough to soften the harsh contours of her countenance. Light hazel eyes, with the same directness as her brother's, looked out of a face with prominent cheekbones and a strong jawline. On her brother the features were powerful. On Rob, as she was always called, they seemed severe, made more so by the fact that her dark brown hair was pulled back in a single braid that hung almost to the waist of her jeans.

Snapping a rawhide quirt against her thigh, she paced off several steps in front of an arched fireplace wide enough to roast a whole cow in. Mounted above it, observing the comings and goings in the large, cluttered main room, was an enormous buffalo head.

At one time the ranch headquarters must have been a showplace, but in this century it had gone to seed. The fat easy chairs, perfect for curling up and reading, were almost threadbare. Dust coated everything. Humans, dogs and cats had tracked mud from the hallway to the main room. Hay flecked the soiled carpet. The house smelled of old rawhide, accented by manure.

Rob gave an impatient snort, then said, "Well, come on. I'll show you your quarters. After you change out of that—" she waved the quirt at Marianna's tailored two-piece silk suit "—you can help old Red Eye throw together some supper."

Their quarters, in one of a half-dozen or so adobe bunkhouses, weren't that bad, especially not when compared to the prison cell Marianna had just vacated. The main room was a combination kitchen, dining room and living room. The furniture was rustic, handmade of pine, the stove and refrigerator antiquated, and the sink still operated by a hand pump. The beds in the two tiny bedrooms looked a lot more comfortable than her former cell's steel frame covered by a thin mattress.

And the bathroom...oh, how Marianna had longed for a real bath in place of the prison's open shower room. And here, alongside a toilet with a pull chain and an old-fashioned pedestal sink, was a huge claw-foot tub of the kind commonly used in the late 1800s. It had an oak rim and brass fixtures. Well, tonight, after dinner, she would indulge herself, soaking for hours in this reminder of lost wealth, until the prison smell was washed away from her hair and skin.

Shyloh went first to her own bedroom, then back to the kitchen, marveling at the mechanics of the hand pump. Marianna began unpacking, setting aside a simple skirt and top to change into for dinner.

"Where's the television, Mom?" Shyloh called.

Marianna sighed. This was going to be quite an experience for her daughter, too. "There isn't one."

Shyloh wandered back into the bedroom to watch Marianna change. "What do they do around here, then?"

"Work."

Marianna's head snapped up at the sound of the deep, resonant voice, and her fingers froze on the panty hose she was smoothing up one calf.

Tom was standing in the bedroom doorway, his big body braced against the doorjamb. The reflection of the lamplight in his eyes made it look as if little fires were burning in them.

"What are you doing in my bedroom?" she demanded. Quickly she smoothed her skirt down over her thigh.

"Your bedroom?" he drawled amiably. "I was under the impression that this piece of property belonged to me."

She should have foreseen that her status here at Mescalero would be no better than it had been in the penitentiary. She was a common criminal, with no privileges, no property, no privacy. Straightening, she expelled a long, steady breath. "You wanted something?"

Her show of strength didn't fool him for a moment. "I thought I'd let you know how things were run here. After you do the dinner dishes, your evening's your own. But mornings start early. 4:30. Mescalero's not one of your European guest resorts. We don't believe in coddling anybody."

"Mr. Malcolm, I'm accustomed to rising at 5:30 in order to be on the set by 6:30. I'm certain I won't have any trouble awakening an hour earlier."

"Good. You can report to the barn first thing." He glanced at Shyloh. "School bus comes at seven. Think you can make it?"

She gave him a timid nod, but his narrowed gaze had already strayed back to Marianna. He looked her over from head to toe. He was frowning slightly, the way a man will do when he's examining a filly he's thinking of buying. "I'd suggest a change of clothing. Say a serviceable pair of jeans and a shirt. You're going to work in the kitchen this evening, not attend a press conference."

Eyes narrowed, she watched him leave. Six months. Could she last that long? Of course she could, when the alternative was seven years behind bars and the loss of her daughter. With a sigh, she changed again, wondering whether Tom Malcolm would call her concho-studded jeans serviceable.

"Mom, can I wear my jeans, too?"

Marianna glanced back at her daughter, who was already struggling out of her corduroy jumper. For Shyloh this was all a marvelous adventure. "Sure, babe, but put on a sweater so you don't get cold."

The sun was already sliding down the far side of the Potrillo Mountains by the time Marianna had dressed again. The late-afternoon air had grown chillier, and with Shyloh skipping ahead she walked briskly across the yard to the ranch house. The owl roosting in the mesquite hooted twice in welcome, and the dog Marianna had noticed earlier trotted out to sniff Shyloh's outstretched hand.

"That's D.O.G," a voice called out.

Both Shyloh and Marianna turned toward a sycamore tree some distance away where a boy—no, a teenager—sat astride what Marianna surmised was an Appaloosa. She had had experience only with Thoroughbreds, but the horse's distinctive markings supported her guess. Another horse, a buckskin, stood nearby, grazing on ragged tufts of buffalo grass that struggled for survival in the sand.

"D.O.G.?" Marianna asked.

"Yeah," the boy said. "For 'Dog.' We spell it out. He doesn't know he is one. Part dog, part coyote, really. Hey, you wanna ride?" he asked Shyloh.

"You serious?" Shyloh asked. "For real?"

The boy, who appeared to be around sixteen years old, grinned, and Marianna thought she had never seen such an engaging smile. The lingering sunlight reflected a warm red tint in his brown hair. "For real."

"Wow!" Shyloh said, starting toward the horses.

Marianna caught up with her. What if he, like herself, was a prisoner on service duty? An inner voice forced her to be fair and ask, What if he, like you, isn't a criminal?

"Here, give me your hand," the boy said, holding out his hand to Shyloh. "Name's Rand. Rand Malcolm."

Shyloh stretched her hand up to him. "What's your horse's name?"

"Ranger." Shyloh hadn't held tightly enough, and Rand bent down to latch on again.

Only then did Marianna notice another boy who was leaning indolently against the tree. He wasn't as old as Rand, maybe fourteen or so. His hair was an Indian black, and instead of Western boots he wore high moccasins with knee-high leggings over them. Their beautiful beadwork caught her interest, and she would have asked him about it, but his strange, quiet manner didn't encourage her.

He stepped forward and cupped his hands for her daughter's foot. "Up you go." There was none of Rand's open friendliness in his voice. Still, it had a surprising maturity to it, a velvety deepness. "No, the other foot." He spoke softly, as if he were calming a spooked pony.

With trepidation, Marianna observed as her daughter swung up behind Rand. "Uh, maybe you shouldn't go riding just yet, Shyloh, until you've had time for proper lessons."

"It's all right, ma'am," Rand said. "Colt and me'll watch her real good."

Shyloh's expression appeared a little uncertain to Marianna, who said, "I don't know...."

"Now's as good a time as any," a man said behind her. She didn't even bother to look around. By now she recognized that chamois-smooth baritone voice.

"The first rule of riding is never to grab the saddle pommel in front of witnesses," Tom Malcolm told Shyloh. "But Rand doesn't count. His saddle pommel has teeth marks in it from when holding on with both hands wasn't enough."

Shyloh giggled, and Rand called, "Awww, Dad!"

Marianna watched the three ride out of the yard. Only then did she turn to face Tom Malcolm. He was toting a saddle, its heavy bulk slung easily over one shoulder. His hat brim shaded his face, except for his lower jaw, which was beard-shadowed this late in the day, and the unlighted cigar anchored at the corner of his mouth.

"Mr. Malcolm, there are certain things you should know. My daughter has a heart murmur and—"

He started off toward the barn and tack room. "And if that doesn't kill her, your overprotectiveness will," he said without looking back. "I suggest you report to the kitchen, Miss McKenna."

"Your suggestion stinks," she said beneath her breath, furious at her position, which didn't permit her to speak her mind aloud.

The kitchen was a mess, with utensils and cartons scattered haphazardly around. Dirty dishes were mounded in the sink. Enormous cauldrons, glass baking dishes and earthenware containers littered the dull orange-tiled counters. Copper and brass saucepans, looking as if they had never been used, hung from the blackened vigas, or rafters. The formerly white stucco walls were now equally as smudged. One wall was taken up by a yard-wide grill and two ovens, none of which appeared to have had a recent cleaning.

An old woman, her long gray hair straggling around her shoulders, labored over roast pork that looked more mangled than shredded. A food-stained apron enveloped her bony frame. A radio was playing festive Mexican music, and the old woman didn't hear Marianna's approach until she was only a few steps away.

Suddenly the woman spun around, the butcher knife she held raised to the level of Marianna's throat.

Dear God, what had she gotten herself into?

"Hot damn!" a gravelly voice exclaimed. "A woman! A damn fine woman!"

Barely daring to breathe, Marianna stared into the seamed face of an old man! There was no doubt of that once she saw the hard-edged features—the fierce, half-hooded eyes, the hawklike nose, the wide, flat cheekbones and granite chin. Without a doubt the features of an Indian. "You're . . . you're Red Eye?"

"What's left of him." He cackled, then sobered to instant dignity. His face seemed centuries old, yet also young.

"At least that's what I'm called by the white nation. Chief Red Eye of the Mescalero Apaches. Leader of many great battles against the enemy, the palefaces with thunder sticks who stole our land, whose forked tongues made promises they broke."

His gravel-mixer voice took on a sonorous quality and, still brandishing the knife, he lifted his arms dramatically, as if in supplication to the heavens. "As a young brave I smoked the peace pipe with Geronimo, and as a warrior I counted coup on General Custer before—"

She began laughing. It felt good to laugh again. "Now why is it that I have the distinct impression you're trying to put one over on me, Red Eye?"

He lowered his arms and winked conspiratorially. "'Cause you're one hot damn smart woman."

"Not that smart," she said grimly, "or I wouldn't be doing KP on a ranch in the middle of nowhere." She glanced at the vegetables—onions, tomatoes, chillies—clumped on a chopping block. "Want to put me to work?"

"Mmm, not so good, a woman convict on Mescalero." He put down the knife and opened a cabinet stocked with herbs and condiments. His gnarled hands withdrew a bottle of vanilla. Head back, he downed a walloping gulp. Then he squinched his wrinkled lids, gave his shaggy head a quick shake and cleared his throat. "Ah, much better! Now, what were we talking about?"

"Putting me to work?" she ventured. "That stuff's not good for you, you know."

"All liquor made to be drunk. Here, make tortillas."

She looked at the mass of dough lumped on a floured wooden slab. Maybe making tortillas was like making pizza crust. She fervently hoped so. She washed her hands and dug into the blob of cornmeal. At the end of half an hour, she had flattened a dozen tortillas to the size and pliability of Frisbees, and Red Eye had finished off another bottle of vanilla. By now she could guess the source of his name.

Red Eye tossed the latest empty vanilla bottle into an unused cauldron and cast a critical glance at the results of her efforts. "Not so good. We eat cantaloupe instead."

She put her hands on her hips and eyed him narrowly. "Red Eye, does Mr. Malcolm or his sister have any idea how much vanilla you drink?"

"Lots, huh?" He grunted in disgust. "Rob took away the cough syrup and mouthwash, and Tom won't take me with him to cantina anymore. Younger people have no respect for their elders. Damn fine shame!"

While they worked, she subtly questioned Red Eye about the Mescalero operation. Not that she learned that much. The old Indian talked freely, but not indiscreetly, in butchered English. From what little she could glean, Mescalero's finances were in a sad state, and Tom, as the major owner of the cattle operation, took in working convicts in exchange for bed and board paid by the state.

At present it seemed that such workers at Mescalero were herself and a young man Red Eye called Bronco Bobby, a dropout druggie who had been on the ninety-section cattle ranch for three years now—two years longer than his sentence. She supposed he must like the place, though she couldn't imagine why.

Red Eye didn't appear to be any more adept at cooking for a crowd than she was. Somehow, though, they finished preparing the meal just as two ranch hands and the rest of the Malcolm family tramped through the doorway into the dining room, which had a lovely T-shaped oak table and buffet whose surfaces had been dulled by years of careless use.

She noticed that the men cast her surreptitious glances. What had Tom told them about her? She was concerned about Shyloh, but then was relieved to see her seated between Rand and Colt, chattering animatedly. Just how did the proud Indian boy fit into the family picture? Was he related to Red Eye? His grandson, perhaps?

Apparently Shyloh didn't find anything unusual in her mother serving food to others, but then, Marianna reflected, her daughter had always accepted her mother's out-of-the-ordinary job as commonplace, too. Shyloh doubtlessly viewed this as just another of her mother's roles.

As one by one everyone took a seat, including old Red Eye, laconic conversation about the day's events began to crisscross the table. Marianna, moving back and forth between the kitchen and dining room, caught snatches of the chitchat.

"...break the ice up in Castle Canyon tomorrow morning..."

"Come winter, I always have to hear the old codgers yap about how much worse the winter of '29 was, or the winter of '37. This winter they just shut their traps."

"...could pack in salt and supplemental feed."

A leathery ranch hand with a grizzled beard, the one who had commented on the old codgers and hard winters, said, "A hunter must have left the Castle Canyon gate open, Tom." The man's eyes blinked continually as he talked. "All eighty head got into the deep-end pasture."

"That's two weeks' work wasted, Emmitt," Tom growled. He glanced pointedly from the too-thick tortillas to Marianna.

She ignored his derisive look and poured tea into the fruit-jar glass of the second ranch hand presumably her fellow convict. His black slouch hat, with its frayed turkey feather, made it difficult for her to judge his age. He glanced up at her, and she caught the glint of a gold earring in one ear. He couldn't have been more than twenty-six or seven.

Grinning suggestively at her, he said, "Well, now, Mr. Malcolm, you sure did a bang-up job in your latest rehabilitation effort."

He was missing both front teeth, she noticed. It was a shame, because he had beautiful brown eyes. He was a good-looking man—if he didn't smile!

"Take your hat off at the table, Bobby." Tom's voice was even, but there was a note of command in it that Bobby obeyed.

Next Tom turned his piercing eyes on her. "Sit down with the rest of us, Miss McKenna. Colt, get her a chair."

Marianna felt the inquisitive stares of the others, but calmly seated herself in the hard-backed chair that Colt politely wedged for her between Rob and Red Eye. Red Eye ate steadily, but Rob studied her with a wariness that bordered on disdain.

Rand broke the strained silence. "It's true what Shyloh says? You really are *the* Marianna McKenna? The movie star?"

With all eyes on her, she felt uncomfortable. Everyone had always assumed that her polished presence was inbred, but they were wrong. As a daughter of a State Department officer who had kept moving to exotic places like Pakistan, Sudan and Somalia, she had constantly suffered the "new kid in school" syndrome. Eventually she had learned to hide her shyness and insecurity behind a serenely composed facade. At UCLA she had discovered that acting enabled her to express herself without any accompanying anxiety.

She lifted her chin and purposefully let her gaze move from one face to another along the table. "I don't know if I would call myself a movie star, but I

am an actress. And—'' she paused and met Tom's
cool, watchful eyes ''—I am not now nor was I ever a
user or distributor of drugs.''

Bobby perked up and waggled his brows wickedly.
''Someone mention drugs?''

''If these are tortillas,'' Emmitt grumbled, ''I'll
scarf down Bronco Bobby's hat, feather and all.''

A ranch of derelicts, Marianna thought. And now
I'm one of these castoffs.

Tom lit up a new cigar and settled back, his elbows
propped on the splintery bleacher behind him, his long
legs stretched out on the one in front. He crossed his
boots, and the big rowels of his spurs made a soft jin-
gling noise in the dead quiet of the night. Midnight
had already made its appearance, but he wasn't sleepy.
The old restlessness was hounding him.

It was a true hunter's moon tonight—red-gold near
the horizon, then shrinking to a silver dollar as it rose.
Its cold light drenched an empty arena that had seen
better days. Ghosts from rodeos past galloped silently across the arena, taunting Tom for his failure to
revive the grandeur that had once been Mescalero's.
Over the years, Teddy Roosevelt and General ''Black
Jack'' Pershing, as well as the Chicago White Stock-
ings, who had held spring training in nearby Fay-
wood, had participated in Mescalero's ongoing
festivities.

But bad investments by his father, falling beef prices
and Tom's own divorce had undermined the finances
of the Mescalero Cattle Company. No longer did the

inhabitants of the surrounding countryside, or cities like El Paso and Tucson and Albuquerque, stream in for barbecues and dances at the gazebo, swimming parties, hayrides and hunting expeditions. Instead, convicted criminals now helped support the day-to-day ranch operations. And not even enough of those to get all the work done.

Tom's teeth ground down on the cigar. Did he really think he was helping rehabilitate a world gone mad? Did he really think he was easing Anita Kahze's restless spirit?

Spirits... ghosts. Had reminiscing about the past evoked the woman who drifted now from the back door toward the gazebo? She was like a fairy fantasy from a make-believe world. Unsubstantial, artificial, lacking the strength of Grandmother Ella, who had converted a mere cattle ranch into one of the showplaces of the Southwest.

Nevertheless, the fantasy was one that could tantalize any man's dreams: a silver-eyed siren... lovely, sparkling, with fiery hair that belied her calm, distant poise. An experienced sophisticate, a savvy lady with a quality all her own.

Yet he'd bet the proceeds from the sale of a Charolais bull that she would be a hellcat if she were ever riled sufficiently.

His mind's eye summoned the sight of the smooth white thigh she'd exposed as she'd slid one long, graceful leg into a pair of hose. She was as lovely and neat as her tailored silk suit, with the creamy skin of a true redhead. Fortune smiles with bared teeth, he thought.

He permitted himself to give in to the attraction he felt for a few magical moments and rose to follow her to the gazebo. His nostrils detected the faint trail of her cigarette smoke before his eyes picked out her silhouette and the pale glow of her lighted cigarette.

His spurs gave him away. She whirled as he stepped through the arched doorway. She was wearing a denim jacket draped over her shoulders against the night's deep cold. Even his untutored eye could tell that the jacket was no department-store purchase. The hand-sewn conchos scattered across the shoulders labeled it a costly little garment, like the matching jeans.

He didn't say anything, and neither did she, but he noticed that her hands gripped the wooden railing behind her. Her face, he noted, was more round than oval, not really classically beautiful. In the silence her disturbed breathing, mingling with her cigarette smoke, drifted in frosty wisps from her parted lips.

"Don't even think about it," he said at last.

She regarded him warily. "About what?"

"About running."

"From you?"

"No. For the border."

"How do you know that's what I was thinking?"

His spurs jangled on the plank floor as he moved to within touching distance of her. The chilly breeze blew her hair toward him. He rested one hip on the railing near her and took the cigar from between his clamped lips. "It's the first thing that crosses every convict's mind on arriving here: only twenty miles to the Mexican border and freedom.''

She tore her gaze away from his face and stared southward. ''If I decided to run,'' she said quietly, ''you couldn't stop me. There's too much border too close.''

''I can track a scorpion across the badlands.''

She looked over her shoulder at him and arched one winged brow. ''I suppose Red Eye taught you to track humans?''

''No,'' he said, feeling the weariness of the day stealing over him. ''A skill left over from Vietnam. And if I don't get you, there are other things out in that vast wasteland that will. Cougars. Sunstroke. Freezing cold. The border patrol.''

Her lips compressed. She pulled her jacket more tightly around her, emphasizing her tiny waist and the hourglass figure that was almost voluptuous despite her slender build. ''You don't have to worry. I'm not going to run away. If it was just me . . .
But I can't take the chance of losing my daughter.''

''Did you do it?'' he asked suddenly. ''Did you smuggle the heroin into the country?'' She would lie, of course. People in her profession always did.

He watched her wide-set gray eyes, which were both intriguing and expressive. They never wavered from his. Their silver centers glittered like the winter night's white-hot stars. ''Would you believe me if I denied it?''

He shrugged. ''Try me.''

Her hands were clenched around the rail. She bowed her head, breathed deeply, then stared off at the distant mountains. "There's not that much to tell," she began in a faint voice. "Three months ago I returned from L.A., where I was dubbing my last film, to the El Paso International Airport. Apparently I instructed the porter to pick up the wrong piece of luggage."

She turned toward him. "I swear it was a mistake! The piece matched the rest of my set, and at a quick glance the bag looked like mine."

Unconsciously she had placed a beseeching hand on his arm. Heat erupted inside him, making him angry with her and even angrier with himself. "Go on."

She sighed bitterly. "By the time I discovered my error, two DEA agents were greeting me politely. They didn't buy my story that the luggage wasn't mine. And after the trial, the jury didn't buy my lawyers' assertion that it was a terrible mix-up. The fact that I was an actress, that I had been married to a rock star, merely added fuel to the district attorney's case and convinced a jury that was already predisposed to convict me on my appearance alone."

"It must be hell being good-looking," he said derisively.

She flared up at him, her voice tense and quiet. "Believe me, many times over the past thirty-four years I've regretted whatever it is that others seem to find attractive in my face. You can't even begin to imagine the envy and animosity it's caused, but this has to be the worst, the ultimate." She looked up at him, tears glistening in her eyes. "To be unjustly convicted of smuggling heroin . . ."

He rose to his feet and stretched. The restlessness within him had ebbed. "I can understand why you've been nominated for an Oscar. Your performance is magnificent."

She gave a hurt little cry, and her palm lashed out at him. The impact smarted against his jaw. He grabbed her wrist and jerked her up against him. "Do that again and I turn you back over to the Feds."

"You wouldn't!"

He looked down into her fascinating gray eyes, lovely even without makeup. They would be winter-cold, he thought. One icy winter he'd burned brush for several hours, and when he'd sifted the ash with his pitchfork, he'd found unmelted snow underneath, where the cold heart of the flames had been. Her eyes would be like that.

"When you've been here long enough, darlin', you'll realize there isn't anything I wouldn't do."

"You're hurting me," she whispered, her lips trembling.

He released her arm, and for a moment they glared at each other. "You can't stand not to be in control, can you?" she fired at him. Then she pushed past him. He watched her flee the gazebo, wondering how she had managed to find his Achilles' heel.

Even with her hair pulled severely back, he had to admit that her face had had a soft, disturbing quality.

He'd always heard that the West was hell on horses and women. As far as he was concerned, it was hell on the institution of marriage, too. He'd learned that firsthand. Yet here was this magical creature with her inviting womanliness and swaying breasts that inflamed his senses—and she was his captive. She could only mean trouble. And he'd had enough woman trouble in his life.

He should have refused to take custody of Marianna McKenna. It would be better for him all the way around if she *did* run away.

Chapter 3

Only vampires returning to their crypts should be up and about at this time of the morning. The light seeping through the small bedroom window was cold and blue. Yawning, Marianna struggled into her jeans and denim jacket. Makeup could wait until six, when she returned to awaken Shyloh for school. A quick glance in the bathroom's tarnished mirror made her feel naked without the layers of makeup she usually wore for filming, but she also felt a certain amount of glorious freedom.

There it was again. That word. Freedom.

Outside, she found not even a promise of daylight on the starlit horizon. False dawn, she thought. In L.A., the city lights drowned out that natural phenomenon. The predawn chill wrapped frosty tentacles around her. Her hair was still damp from the

invigorating shower. "Brr," she muttered, shivering.
Who would have thought the desert of the Southwest
could be so cold? It was even colder now than it had
been last night.

Last night.

The encounter with Tom Malcolm had played havoc
with her sleep. She usually used finesse to achieve
whatever she needed from her co-workers, who were
by nature temperamental. But Tom wasn't temperamental; he was unrelentingly autocratic—and he didn't
respond to finesse.

With his detached self-command, he was a kind of
feudal lord of his range principality, accustomed to
riding roughshod over people. Obviously she was no
exception. Theirs was a primal relationship. His implacable manner threatened, even repelled her, yet she
found herself darkly fascinated by him.

Summoning fortitude, she hurried across the yard,
past the machine shed toward the barn. Overhead,
barn swallows swooped, outlined in dark crescents
against the lightning sky, like boomerangs. She followed them as they led her toward the barn, then
slipped into the warm interior.

She didn't know exactly who she was supposed to
report to, but she certainly hadn't expected so much
activity to be going on inside. Men were coming and
going. Colt toted an armload of baled hay. Rand
carted a saddle blanket and saddle. Emmitt came out
of the tack room carrying a bridle. He glanced at her
and muttered to himself, "Pancakes gotta be better
than tortillas."

"Hey, pretty woman," Bobby called out. He was zipping on tanned batwing chaps. "Need some help? I'm the man for you."

He said it so good-naturedly that she couldn't take offense. Besides, even with that toothless smile he was appealing, even cute. "I'm looking for Mr. Malcolm, or his sister."

"I'm in here." The voice belonged to Rob.

Marianna found the young woman at the back of the barn, where two stalls had been combined into one. Her shapeless felt hat had been tugged down low, hiding her long hair, and she wore men's overalls under a bulky plaid woolen jacket. She was sitting on a stool, milking a cow that switched its tail contentedly. "Ever done this?" she asked Marianna.

Marianna shook her head, her eyes trained on the stream of milk that hissed into the pail.

Rob grimaced. "You're not good for much around here, are you?" She went back to kneading an udder. Marianna watched, fascinated, as steam rose from the pail's contents. "Well, gather the eggs and start breakfast," Rob said without looking back at Marianna. "Red Eye is out of whack again this morning."

Bobby stuck his head inside the stall. "What she means is that old Red Eye found another cache of rotgut."

Marianna caught up with Bobby outside the stall. "Chickens?"

He made a bow and swept his feathered hat low. "This way to the henhouse, milady."

At least someone around here had a sense of humor, she thought. She followed him out behind the barn. The air was warming, and dewdrops sparkled like individual diamonds on the blades of grass. The stars were growing fainter overhead, which was the one place she shouldn't have been looking. Twice she stepped in cow patties and had to pause to knock the clumps off her tennis shoes. Now she knew why cowboys wore boots.

"Usually Red Eye fixes breakfast," Bobby was saying, "but every so often he gets liquored up."

A chicken-wire pen surrounded the henhouse, a corrugated shed that looked as if it were about to collapse in on itself. Her nostrils wrinkled at a faint, unpleasantly familiar odor. "What is that?"

Bobby laughed. "Last week I managed to shoot a skunk just outside the henhouse, and his memory is with us whenever the wind's right."

Inside, she welcomed the smell of musty straw. Chickens greeted them with disapproving clucks and flapping wings. Bobby turned on a light switch, and the room was shafted with dust particles and drifting feathers.

From the corner of her eye she spotted a ring-tailed cat picking its way agilely over the mounded straw to leave the henhouse.

"That's Phrank," Bobby said. "With a *Ph*. 'Pears we disturbed his napping place."

"Interesting animal names you've got here." She followed Bobby over to the far wall. "Is Red Eye going to be all right?"

He removed a wicker basket from a peg. "You have to understand, ma'am, that Red Eye has the idea that liquor is to be drunk." He snatched an egg from an unoccupied nest, adding, "And he acts accordingly."

One sitting hen wasn't too pleased when Marianna tried to reach under it, and it pecked her hand. She decided to abandon her quest for that particular egg.

"Now as for Red Eye," Bobby continued, "the RPM of his Adam's apple, when properly accelerated by *aguardiente* flowing over his tonsils, is only a few beats shy of that of the wing of a hummingbird in full flight."

She had to chuckle. Bobby might be a dropout druggie, but he was obviously educated. She definitely liked his wry sense of humor.

At the creaking of the door hinges, she straightened and turned to find Tom's glance moving from her to Bobby, whose hand appeared to be closed immediately over hers on the basket handle.

With an almost imperceptible jerk of his head, Tom signaled the young man.

"Gotcha, Mr. Malcolm," Bobby said, grinning cheerfully. He tipped his hat and swaggered past Tom.

When he was gone, Tom turned his full attention to her. His dark gaze lingered a moment at the apex of her thighs, where the denim of her jeans was pulled taut. She watched his observant eyes move upward to settle on her flushed face. She wished now that she had worn makeup and done something about her hair.

"Doesn't take you long, does it?"

Basket in hand, she faced him. "Just what are you insinuating?"

He ambled over to stand directly in front of her. His hard mouth clamped down on the cigar as his eyes squinted down at her. "Stirring up the ranch hands."

"I did nothing of the kind! I was merely laughing at something Bobby said. Is that supposed to be provocative or something?"

He hooked his thumbs inside his low-slung belt, where he had tucked a pair of split-cowhide gloves. She followed the movement and stared at his hands, then realized where they had fallen and looked away, embarrassed. His stance and the cut of his fringed chaps were sexually suggestive, and she licked suddenly dry lips. No wonder, she thought distractedly, that the cowboy was considered supremely male.

"The way *you* laugh," he growled, "yes. It *is* provocative."

She could feel all the old anger bubbling inside her. "It's because I'm an actress, isn't it? You think the acting profession is only slightly better than prostitution."

"It's because you're too damned tempting." He shoved his hat back on his forehead and glowered down at her. "This is never going to work."

She could feel it coming, and the threat of being sent back to prison made her tremble all over. The basket dropped from her sweat-slick hands. Eggs rolled between their feet. Mortified, she abruptly squatted on her heels to collect the eggs. Tom did the same, and an egg cracked beneath his mud-caked boot. Her gaze flew from the squashed yolk matting the straw to his hard-edged face.

"I'm sorry!" she blurted. "Here, let me get them." Rapidly she began retrieving the eggs. "I'm not usually so clumsy. It's just—"

Tom's large hand closed over hers. She went absolutely still. The scent of old leather and tobacco tantalized her nostrils. Slowly she raised her gaze to stare questioningly into his unyielding eyes, where time had done its calligraphy on their corners.

"It won't work," he repeated. "You'll have to go."

She wanted to babble that she would do anything to stay, anything to keep from going back to that cell, anything to keep from losing Shyloh. She would have been willing to grovel, but she knew that wouldn't get her anywhere with a man like Tom. She straightened her back and stared back at him with all the calmness she could muster.

"It's not the ranch hands you're worried about, is it?" she asked. "It's yourself."

For a long moment his angry gaze dueled with her challenging one. "Cowboying's always been a man's world. When a woman enters she's intruding, creating an awkward situation."

"I'd be willing to wager that your sister would argue that point."

Frowning, he lifted her hand and turned it over. She stood transfixed as his finger traced the smooth pads of her palm. "What do you think these hands will look like after six months of hard labor?" The harsh impatience in his voice belied his gentle touch.

With his other hand he traced the contour of her cheek where it swept up into her hairline. She trembled beneath his callused touch. "What happens to this fair skin once the wind and sun and sand have had their way with it?" He paused and, with the rock-hard gaze of a gunfighter, searched her eyes. "I won't be responsible for what happens. Will you?"

She understood exactly what he was alluding to. If he thought he could unnerve her, he was mistaken. "Yes, Mr. Malcolm. A thousand times, yes!"

Rob spun away from the henhouse doorway. A dull ache thudded in her temples. Tom and that actress. Could there be anything...? No, impossible. Ever since Vivian had left Tom had been turned off by city-slicker women. Long before that, even.

Still fretting, Rob strode back to the barn. She stopped before a stall gate with a pedigree mounted behind plastic identifying the occupant as the filly Apache Belle, out of the famed King Ranch quarter horse stud, Three Bar. Of all the cutting horses she had raised, broken and trained, Apache Belle held the most promise.

At one time she had known promise of another sort. As a girl, Rob had barrel raced in rodeos, and she had been good. There had been the promise of prize money in that, but with her teenage years she had continued to grow taller and taller and, with her increasing height, more awkward. Tall girls normally didn't do well in barrel racing.

She entered the stall and rubbed her cheek against the dun's velvety-soft muzzle. The worst of the winter was past—she hoped—and the filly, leggy and fine like a running horse, had begun to shed its winter coat. It nickered, and its breath on Rob's hand was warm and moist and sweet, like fresh grass.

"You'll be the one, Apache Belle. You'll earn me that million-dollar purse."

Then Tom wouldn't have to work so hard, Rob thought, turning up her collar against the morning's rising wind as she left the barn for the ranch house. Tom owned three-fourths of the Mescalero Cattle Company and she owned the other fourth, and she often felt she wasn't doing her share. She felt that her brother had to shoulder too much of the load—making a working cattle spread out of both his portion and hers. So far her cutting-horse operation had brought in only nickels and dimes.

The old house was toasty-warm. Rob loved it and the memories it held. She shrugged out of her coat and hung it on the hall tree. The pungent aroma of percolating coffee and frying venison sausage wafted to her. She followed the sound of masculine chatter and chuckles. In the main room everyone was seated around the long table. Her gray eyes roamed over the gathering: proud young Colt; dear old grumbling Emmitt, as jackrabbit-lean as ever; the young stud Bobby; sensitive Rand; and incorrigible, rank old Red Eye. His hangover this morning inflamed his eyeballs, making them into fierce, glowing red orbs.

Her gaze passed by Shyloh to settle on Tom, dominating everyone from the head of the table. Over the rim of his coffee cup, he winked at her. His hair was flecked with gray, and the groove at one corner of his mouth was cut more deeply than ever. But his eyes glowed, and his mouth had lost nothing of its humor and virility.

For as long as she could remember, since her mother's death when Rob had been three, she had been surrounded by men: her father and Tom, along with her nephews, ranch hands and, of course, old Red Eye. Then, too, there had been the occasional rehab convicts Tom had taken on. Until yesterday, they had all been men, too.

Her eyes narrowed on the woman cooking pancakes at the stove. Her movements had a quiet, elegant grace. Her store-new jeans and ribbed sweater didn't conceal her softly feminine curves. Rob thought of her own worn-out jeans, which were army surplus—and of her hands.

Last month, one finger had lost a nail when it had gotten pinched in the tailgate of the pickup from which she had been scattering feed cakes to the cows. Her hands were callused and scarred, her fingernails bitten. There were recent cuts she'd gotten when she had been busting open a frozen pond last week and fallen on her hands and knees on the ice in front of a belligerent bull.

She studied Marianna's perfectly groomed hair, her long, polished fingernails and freshly applied make-up, and wondered what on earth this place was coming to. Even as she watched, Marianna burned a finger on the cast-iron skillet. With a small muttered "Ouch," she made a fanning motion with her hand, then daintily sucked on the injured fingertip.

Scorn for such a womanly gesture, scorn for womanly weaknesses in general, curled the ends of Rob's long mouth. The smile gradually froze into a rictus of amazement as she saw the smoldering gaze in Tom's eyes. Her glance ricochetted back to the recipient of that gaze, and little alarm signals went off inside her.

Colt Kahze was built lean and compact, like a mustang, so one didn't notice his size at first. The boy sat easy in the saddle, and that was all he did. He just let the horse twist and shake its head. He kept it walking for a while, circling the corral, then rode back to the gate.

"I heard Indians are good with horses."

Colt's dark eyes studied the frail girl who had climbed on the lower railing to watch him. She stared up at him with unabashed curiosity. Where had her shyness gone? The crisp afternoon had put color in her cheeks. It was the first time in the week she had been at Mescalero that he had seen any sign of life in her. With her hair the color of moonlit grass, she always looked washed out.

"I guess you heard a lot of things about Indians. What I know about gentling, though, I learned from Tom."

"You been here long?"

"Most of my life."

"How come you don't go to school?"

"I do."

"I haven't seen you go this week."

"I go to the Mescalero Indian Day School. Up on the reservation."

"Oh." She hauled herself up to perch on the top railing. "Will you teach me to ride?"

"It Tom says it's all right."

"Is Tom *your* boss, too?"

"He's my father."

Marianna felt that this empty quarter of New Mexico was the only place on earth where a disaster would go unnoticed. There was nothing to be seen—only two turkey vultures perched on the fence posts, wings spread in the heat of the March afternoon. How could the day be so hot when the nights were so cold? This had to be the hottest, driest place in the Southwest. *Despoblado,* old Red Eye called it—the unpopulated place. A land so full of silence that there was no sound. She sat scrunched in Rob's pickup, squeezed between her and Red Eye, who kept nodding off during the interminable twenty-three-mile trip to the local store, which also served as the post office.

The Border Bluff Trading Post, lone survivor of a bygone era, perched on a low ridge overlooking the dry wash of Castalon Creek and the Mexican border. Five generations of clannish ranching families had patronized the trading post. The flat-roofed adobe was one of the few establishments still using the barter system. Its walls retained the scars of the raids of

Pancho Villa. Out on its wide covered porch, dances continued to be held every Saturday night. The festive music drew cowhands, railroad crews, geologists, Mexicans from across the border, roughnecks drilling for oil in the relentless, savage land of the Chihuahuan desert, even the border patrol.

Rob parked her battered blue Dodge near the trading post's single gas pump. Nearby, a big roan, its tail end to the wind, stood tethered to a hitching post. "Ruthie's here."

From Rob's tone, Marianna gathered that this information was of some importance.

Red Eye, who was wearing a gaudy velveteen shirt and baggy jeans, seemed to perk up. "Beer?"

But Rob was already climbing out of the pickup. Marianna slid out on her side. How could the sun be so hot and the wind so cold? Quickly she caught up with Rob's long strides.

Inside the large, dimly lighted room, glass-fronted cabinets displayed Indian jewelry. Beneath the high ceiling, aisle after aisle contained shelves of hand-woven blankets, saddles and bolts of cloth, as well as canned goods, sacks of pinto beans and cooking utensils. A cast-iron potbellied stove gave off welcome heat. On the wall behind the counter, a neon sign proclaimed Tecate—Se Vende Aquí.

Rob turned to Red Eye. "Remember, no drinking."

Red Eye shook his grizzled head morosely. "Damn fine shame!"

"Help you, Rob?" the leathery-skinned woman behind the counter asked.

"Well?" Rob asked Marianna. The young woman's boot tapped an impatient staccato beat on the concrete-slab floor. "You got the list?"

Marianna reached into the pocket of her denim jacket and withdrew the grocery list she had made early that morning, inexpensive items that would add immeasurably to the quality of the bland meals she had been cooking: dehydrated herbs like parsley, watercress and paprika; a jar of pimiento, if they had it; cans of cream soups—mushroom or broccoli would do for a start. And dinner napkins instead of paper towels!

"Gotten any rain out your way?" the storekeeper asked Rob.

"Not a drop."

Red Eye leaned close to Marianna and asked in a low-pitched, scratchy voice that was a trumpet blast of whiskey, left over from the night before, "Vanilla? You put vanilla on the list?"

Smiling, she waggled her finger at him. "Yes, but I'm hiding the bottle."

"Rob!" A woman emerged from an aisle and came into view. Like Rob, she was dressed in Western attire, but was perhaps seven or eight years older, maybe nearing thirty. Glossy brown hair framed an intelligent face. "I thought I heard your voice. Afternoon, Red Eye."

Red Eye grunted, indicating his feelings about the afternoon.

"Came to do some stocking, Ruthie." Rob glanced significantly at Marianna. "Got us a woman convict to do the cooking these days."

At that moment Marianna wished she could evaporate.

The other woman offered a friendly smile and extended a gloved hand. "Hi. I'm Ruthie. Ruthie Cuddahay."

"Marianna McKenna."

Ruthie's naturally curving brows drew together in puzzlement. "You look familiar." Her expression cleared into one of pure sunshine. "You're the actress, aren't you?"

"She's a convict now."

Ruthie ignored Rob's statement. "Well, welcome to the land God forgot. Believe me, it grows on you. You'll come to love it."

"She's not gonna be here that long," Rob said flatly.

Rob's antagonism took another tack on the trip back to Mescalero. "Ruthie's a widow," she told Marianna.

"Is she?"

"Her spread backs up to ours."

"Really?"

"She's kinda sweet on Tom."

At last Marianna perceived the intent behind Rob's seemingly offhand conversation.

Rob slid her a sidelong glance. "Tom sets a great store by her, too."

Marianna looked her straight in the eye. "Good for him. Look, I'm not plotting to take your place at Mescalero."

Rob returned her gaze to the caliche road. Her mouth was set in a hard line. "No way you could. Before Tom gets his head all turned around, you'll be leaving. You won't last any six months, Miss McKenna. I'll see to that."

Fear shafted through Marianna. Here was another Malcolm who wanted her off Mescalero, although for a different reason. But like her brother, Marianna realized, Rob would be indifferent to pleading. That was a weakness. So determination emphasized every word she spoke. "Oh, but I will last six months, Rob. There's no way you're going to drive me off Mescalero."

Chapter 4

Tom's pencil swiftly tallied the numbers. He figured he had six tons of hay left. He was putting out 165 pounds daily, so with luck he'd have enough for about twenty more days, or through the end of April. There were also about three tons of sweet feed left, and he was down to feeding twenty-five pounds a day.

Ranch mathematics was an overlooked subject. Rand seemed to think his career goal of being a rancher precluded the need to get good grades in high school.

Then there was Colt. The kid wasn't doing well at the reservation school. Tom was tempted to transfer him to the closest public school, the junior high school in Deming. But a gut feeling told him that Colt needed to learn about his own people first, had to figure out where he was coming from before he'd know where he was going.

Colt, who had been all awkward legs as a toddler and just as frisky as his animal namesake, displayed astonishing gentleness with hurt animals. Tom recalled the calf that had lost its tail and ear tips to a bitter winter blizzard. Cold had nursed the calf back to health. Perhaps that was why Tom had agreed to let Colt train under the old shaman after school several days a week. Then again, maybe the kid could make it as a veterinarian—if he could manage to master his studies.

Tom glanced out his office window. A freak winter storm had roared in like the Trans-Siberian Express to throw spring off balance. The scent of lavender and yellow mustard was heavy in the air, while tiny crystal flakes of ice pelted the windowpanes. His muscles felt kinked with sitting. He detested being holed up by bad weather. Rising, he stretched. He had slept restlessly and worked tired. Now he started down the hallway.

From the main room, he heard an "Achoo!"

A cursory glance didn't find anyone. Red Eye? The old Indian usually slept off his hangovers in the pantry, but he might have passed out behind the couch. Tom peeked behind it—and caught a tempting view of the McKenna woman's tantalizing backside. She was on her hands and knees, scrubbing the parquet floor. He couldn't remember the last time the floor had been really cleaned.

She was humming quietly to herself and obviously hadn't heard the soft tread of his spurless boots. For a moment he listened to the soft melody. It was full of a calmness, a gentleness, that was foreign to what he knew about her. Magazine and newspaper articles pictured her as an actress's actress, unswerving in her dedication to her career. Apparently she worked hard—and played hard, if messing around with heroin could be called playing. He would have bet that underneath that cool, poised exterior she was a real firecracker.

Her humming broke off with another "Achoo" and a muttered "Damn," then resumed again.

He began to pass by, then noticed the three rifles in the wall rack. They had been moved. His glance fell on the culprit, who was still humming to herself, unaware of his exasperation. "I told you not to touch the guns."

She jumped, spun around on her knees and stared up at him, her mouth open in surprise. Her face was bruised with fatigue.

"That's one of the rules," he growled. "And if you want to go breaking them, then you can damn well go back!"

"I was just dusting them."

"Dust them and you wipe off all the oil, and then they begin to rust. So just keep your hands off them."

He stalked by her, collected his sheepskin coat and Stetson from the hall tree and went outside. At the banging of the screen door, the owl in the mesquite flapped its wings, as if preparing to take flight.

The wind howled around the corner of the house, so strong that it seemed to blow the air out of his lungs, making it impossible to draw a breath. The ice crystals stung and cut his face. Only fools went out on a day like this, even in a car.

Why did he do it? he asked himself. Certainly no one ranched for the money. It wasn't as if he enjoyed suffering and hardship. It was as though he was honor bound to see this through every season, every crisis. When he succeeded, he felt as if he had accomplished something. And the more difficult or dangerous the circumstance, the greater the exhilaration when it was all over and he had come out triumphant.

Past the vacant bunkhouses, south of the barn, he saw three coyotes trotting along in a businesslike manner, their gray tails lowered. It was their mating season. At night their yelps and ululations always sounded wild and ecstatic, arousing yearnings in him that he strove to tamp down.

At the corral, D.O.G. joined him. Had the animal been yearning, too? Had the wild part of him been longing for a mate among the coyotes? But the dog half of him could no more survive in that wilderness than he himself could in civilization. The McKenna woman's world. She was right, of course, about his need to be in control. Because he was afraid to surrender what little self-control he had left, he had found himself fighting her from the beginning.

The heavy cows, those carrying calves, were bunched up against the fence, heads down. If it began snowing enough for drifts to form, he would have to move them. Their breath could freeze in a solid column of ice from each nostril to the ground, eventually smothering them. At his approach, they turned their heads simultaneously in his direction. Their long eyelashes were outlined with frost, and their eyes stared at him wisely.

"How you doin', darlins?" These were the cows he had crossbred to his Charolais bull, and because it was a larger breed, the birthing could be difficult. If the heavy cows were corralled close to the house, where he could watch them night and day, he could be on hand for the calving and, if he was lucky, save himself a vet bill.

Only one was ready to calve. She was lying quietly, chewing her cud throughout the contractions. She kept looking behind her as if wondering why the calf hadn't been born yet. "Won't be long, old gal," he told her.

He hefted two hay bales from the barn and scattered hay for the cows. Walking in the corral mud required a sort of bowlegged, two-step gait in order to keep his mud-caked feet far enough apart so he wouldn't trip over his own boots. The mud concerned him, because heavy cows had been known to slip in it, go down face first and then, unable to get up, suffocate.

If it wasn't the snow, he reflected on his trip back to the house, then it was the mud.

Preoccupied with the approach of calving, he almost tripped over Marianna, who was scrubbing the floor near the empty wood box. Before long, he mentally noted, he'd have to chop more firewood.

She sat back on her heels and glared up at him. Her titian hair, which had been skewered atop her head, escaped to fall in riotous ringlets over her forehead.

"Do you realize," she gritted between her teeth, "that I've been scrubbing the floors all morning, and you...you are—" she paused, obviously to search for an appropriate word "—are so churlish as to not even bother cleaning the mud from your boots?"

She had a point, but her manner did nothing to lighten his mood. Besides, he knew better than to let an employee have the upper hand. Especially one who was also a convict—and a beautiful woman.

Purposefully he let his gaze slide over the floor, which was polished enough to please even a Windsor. "Looks great—with a little *g*. I want it to look good with a capital *G*. Understand?"

He strode on past her, his boots depositing clumps of mud on the gleaming wooden floor. He got no farther than his office doorway before he felt a soft thud between his shoulder blades. He reached over his shoulder and flicked off the sticky black goo. At the sight of the mud coating his fingers, his eyes widened in disbelief. Slowly he turned to face her. Her expression looked stricken, as if she just realized the enormity of what she had done.

"The military would call that insubordination," he said, returning to her with measured steps.

She jumped to her feet, her hands clenched. "This isn't the military!" she snapped, but her trembling hands betrayed her fear.

"No, but as far as you're concerned, it's still a prison." He stared coldly at her. "I could confine you to your room. Let you do without food for a day." In his fury, he took pleasure in seeing the blood drain from her face. "Or I could—"

"You just try it," she spat. "I'll have the best lawyer in the country down on your—"

Something in him snapped. "Damn it, woman, you're going to learn your place!" He grabbed her shoulders and jerked her to him. For several frozen seconds he held her against him. He felt the tips of her breasts straining against his chest. A hard, demanding ache knotted quickly at his groin. He wanted to make her surrender to him, this proud, defiant woman who thought she was too good for him. He wanted to bruise that strawberry-ripe mouth with furious kisses. He wanted to...

The sound of her gasping breath, loud in the silent room, broke in on thoughts that he had no business entertaining. But how did you shut out an intoxicating fantasy that had suddenly become reality? His mind still grappled in the darkness of the night with the forbidden, with thoughts of this woman who had somehow insinuated herself into his well-ordered life.

Deliberately he scowled at her, and his fingers dug into her soft shoulders as he tried to displace his latent passion, substituting righteous anger instead.

On her face was the look of a cornered animal, braced to meet a captor too dangerous to battle. "I'm sorry," she whimpered, "but please... please, don't hurt me."

He blinked, gathering his scattered senses. "Hurt you?" Suddenly he felt like scum. He set her away from him. "Going back to prison would hurt you worse than anything I could do, so you'd better not provoke me again."

"Provoke you?" she whispered, rubbing one shoulder as if it were tender. "Then don't go out of your way to goad me."

She was back at it again. Playing the grande dame when she was a common criminal. "Now, you listen to me—" Over her shoulder he glimpsed Rob, standing at the other end of the hall, in the kitchen doorway. How long had she been there? And how much had she overheard?

"We'll finish this later," he muttered, and stalked outside again, where he could cool off.

He could only hope he could maintain better control of himself when "later" came, because he had the feeling he had opened a Pandora's box. Even after such brief contact with Marianna McKenna, holding her soft, pliant body against him, feeling the sexual heat she unknowingly gave off, he knew that never again would he be blissfully unaware of her secret and mysterious charms.

For him, the end to her six months' probation couldn't come quickly enough.

God, she ached all over. She hadn't realized she was so out of shape. Housecleaning was more strenuous than she remembered. Just bending over to lift the cast-iron skillet onto the stove taxed her sore muscles.

She sneezed again. Perhaps she was getting the flu. Or perhaps she just hurt from Tom Malcolm's brutal grasp.

The embarrassing thing about it was that she had somehow welcomed his touch, tingled within his powerful hold. Once Jax had hit her—it had been the first and last time. She hadn't been about to enjoy the role of battered wife. She had filed for divorce almost immediately afterward, though in truth the marriage had been on shaky ground from the beginning. It hadn't been all Jax's fault, either. But over the years she had managed to forgive both him and herself.

She went to the pantry for an onion. The first week she hadn't been able to find anything in the oversize pantry. Onions, garlic and potatoes had been mixed haphazardly in slatted wooden boxes partially hidden by institutional-size food cans and flour and sugar sacks. Some of the potatoes and onions had even sprouted.

The day before she had rearranged the pantry, hanging the onions and garlic in net bags and storing only the potatoes in the boxes. The cans were now stacked according to contents.

When she opened the pantry door, a body tumbled out at her feet. She gave a startled gasp that was almost a shriek. Then her hand went to her chest in relief. Red Eye grinned drunkenly up at her from his sprawled position on the floor.

"Come on, Red Eye," she said, bending over him and feeling every bone in her body protesting. "You have to get upstairs to your bedroom before Rob or Tom catches you.''

He held up one gnarled finger. "Don't. Red Eye, the noble shief of the Meshcaleros, can walk on his hown.''

"You can't even talk on your own," she said, hauling him to an upright stance.

His knees wobbled, then locked. He smiled merrily. "Told you sho.''

She watched him lurch away and shook her head doubtfully. Most likely he'd collapse on the sofa before he made it to the stairway. But she knew better than to force her help on the proud old man.

She stepped inside the pantry. Too bad the house had been built before the discovery of electricity, because the pantry certainly could have used a light.

Suddenly all light was eliminated as the pantry door closed on her. She drew in her breath sharply. After those five days of incarceration, she had acquired an aversion to being closed in. She turned the knob, but the door didn't give. She started to shake. She leaned her shoulder into the door and shoved. It gave only slightly. Something heavy was blocking it.

Sweat broke out on her forehead. Her heart hammered loudly, painfully, against her rib cage. She fought to gain control of the terror building in her. "Help!" she called out. "Help me!"

Silence.

All the ranch hands were gone, she knew, but Rob had come inside less than ten minutes before to change her snow-wet clothes. The young woman should have heard her yelling.

She was on the edge of panic. She tried the door again, then rammed her shoulder against it, but she achieved nothing more than a painful bruise. She could feel herself starting to hyperventilate. "Help me!" she cried. "Someone, please help me!"

Tears trickled down her cheeks. She could feel the walls closing in on her, compressing her until she soon would be only a bloody, pulpy mass. She had to get out! Now! She pounded her fists against the door. She screamed and screamed. "Help, please! Get me out of here!"

She collapsed in a heap on the floor, sobbing brokenly, desperately, for how long she didn't know. Her pleas were a frantic litany. "Someone, please, let me out! I can't stand it!"

Abruptly the door was wedged open. She blinked against the sudden light. The Indian boy stood there. At his feet lay a snoring Red Eye. "Are you all right?" Colt asked.

She closed her eyes and nodded. When she opened them again, Colt was rolling Red Eye's inert body away so that the door could open fully.

"Red Eye chooses funny places to sleep," Colt explained with an embarrassed glance at her.

She looked beyond him to see Rob. "What's going on?" the young woman asked innocently.

"You didn't hear me yelling to be let out?" Marianna couldn't believe the woman wouldn't have heard her.

Rob's lips widened into a grin. "Course not. I was showering."

"Achoo! Oh, no."

Marianna wiped her nose with another tissue. Her sniffles appeared to be turning into a full-fledged cold. Every bone in her body ached, but it wasn't due solely to the oncoming cold. It was the hard physical work. She wasn't accustomed to manual labor.

Maybe she could attribute it to her age. Time had always seemed to be speeding past her. Until recently. It was like that in the film business. She had the sense that she should be concentrating on the aroma and texture of the time she was using. Concentrating on the Now. Surprisingly, she hadn't minded aging of late. Within her flowed a feeling, like an underground stream, that aging, reaching forty, might turn out to be a joyous event. One full of new strength and wisdom, as if life were a party she'd been nervous about attending but was finding herself enjoying.

Marianna's mouth twisted. Rob had obviously thrown down the gauntlet with that closet scare. Now it was up to her to figure out how to respond.

The front door banged open with a howling wind, and Shyloh called out, "Mom?"

"Back here, babe."

Her daughter appeared in the bedroom doorway. Her cheeks and nose were reddened from the cold, and her hair looked like yarn that had been tangled by a cat. But some of the frailness that Marianna had always associated with the heart murmur seemed absent. Perhaps it was the open spaces, the fresh air. Or perhaps just the passing of time. The doctor had promised her that most children outgrew the condition.

Shyloh held a blackened old tin coffeepot. "I thought you said it'd be warm here, like California."

Marianna sneezed again and reached for another tissue. "I thought it would be. Red Eye keeps saying this is one of those freak late-winter storms. Happens every seven years or so, he says. What's that you've got?"

Shyloh glanced down at the coffeepot. "Oh, I forgot. Rose-hip tea." She started back toward the kitchen. "Colt made it," she called over her shoulder. "He said it would be good for your cold."

"Anything would be welcome right now," Marianna called back. She felt as if centuries of cold were trying to leach the warmth from her bones.

Shyloh returned with a coffee cup that was chipped and stained from years of use. With the dignity of royalty, she poured tea into it and held it out to Marianna. "Did you know that Mr. Malcolm is Colt's daddy, Mom? Hey, this is like having a tea party, isn't it?"

Marianna almost sloshed the hot tea on herself. "What did you say?"

"A tea party. You know, when I used to play dolls, and you'd—"

"No. About Colt and Mr. Malcolm. Are you sure you understood what you heard?"

Shyloh's fine brows knitted. "Yes, Mom. Colt told me so himself."

"He wasn't talking about Red Eye maybe being his grandfather or something like that?"

"No. He said Mr. Malcolm was his father, I'm sure of it."

"Did he say who his mother is?"

Shyloh shook her head. "Uh-uh. Is the tea good, Mom?"

"Very."

Outside, the wind suddenly stopped. But the eerie silence seemed worse to Marianna. Like the silence in the eye of a hurricane.

Chapter 5

The fierce late-April sunlight toasted her arms and the back of her neck, though it was still early, not yet six. The patio thermometer read eighty-eight degrees, warm enough to go swimming—if the free-form pool's cracked tiles were fixed and it was filled with water.

She shifted the basket of eggs she had gathered to her other arm and stooped to peer at the fragile-looking Indian paintbrush pushing through the arid sand. Above, a barn swallow whistled close to her, trailing horsehair to weave into its nest. She smiled to herself and rose to return to the house. Spring was certainly making itself felt—to the point that the yearling heifers in the south pasture had attracted the attention of five bulls, which were all lined up along the fence, staring avidly.

One bull, satanic-looking with its ridged shoulders
and thick neck, rumbled in its throat threateningly.
The nearest heifer continued to graze, indifferent to
this male attention. Or at least it seemed to be, but
after a moment it switched its tail, then glanced over
its shoulder, reminding Marianna of a high school girl
passing by a football squad running drills.

Marianna sighed almost wistfully and turned her
footsteps toward the ranch house. She had to get
breakfast going before the ranch hands finished their
morning chores. She had barely gotten the biscuits in
the oven when the men began filing to the table. She
knew Tom was among them. The confrontation several days earlier had opened her eyes, made her aware
of him as more than just her jailer.

She had sensed from the start that even though he
was a backcountry rancher he was an intelligent and
independent man. Now she realized that, precisely
because of those qualities, he was much more complicated than she could have imagined. You could love
the man or hate him, but you certainly couldn't walk
away feeling nothing either way.

Without even looking, she was aware of his hot eyes
on her backside as she bent to remove the tray of biscuits.

Then she also became aware of Rob's racking
cough. How fitting if the other woman had caught her
cold!

Behind her, Rand was saying, "Come summer, we
oughta build a garage for all our cars—somewhere the
winter snow won't block the entrance."

With a snort, Emmitt suggested, "Try the Belgian Congo."

"Geez, I feel like I've cracked a rib coughing," Rob gasped.

"Stay in today," Tom ordered.

Marianna took her seat between Shyloh and Bobby.

"Who's gonna help Bobby get the dry cows?" Rob asked, then erupted in another fit of coughing.

Bobby waggled his eyebrows and grinned lecherously. "How about Miss McKenna here? She can help me herd with the pickup."

"You got a crush on my mom?" Shyloh asked with the innocence of youth.

Marianna felt the betraying blush. Bobby was a good seven years or so younger than she was.

"You're going out to herd cows, Bobby," Tom said, his words clipped. "Not get seduced by a woman."

"Now just a moment!" she said, throwing her napkin on the table and jumping to her feet. "I resent what you're implying."

He fixed her with a cold stare. "Sit down."

All eyes but Tom's seemed to find somewhere else to look. For a moment she wavered. Then, glaring back at him, she prudently sat down again.

"Now," he continued in an easy tone that was no less menacing, "you can resent me all you want, but you'll still do as I say."

"Is she *your* woman?" Bobby asked with the masculine petulance of a young man thwarted.

Briefly Tom's eyes met hers across the table. "The court says so." He shifted his hard gaze to Bobby.

"You—I want you shoveling the manure out of the barn as soon as breakfast is over."

Rob's sharp cough interrupted the strained silence. She glanced up apologetically from behind her hand. "I, uh, really don't feel like hazing cows this afternoon, Tom."

He canted his head, his eyes scowling in concern. "You've never let a cold keep you down, Rob."

"Well, er, do you mind if she—" she nodded toward Marianna, as if using her name were more than she could stand "—if she helps Bobby today?"

So, Marianna thought, Rob was trying a different tactic. Wearily she rose and began clearing away the dishes. Everyone seemed glad to escape the breakfast table.

By eleven that morning she was riding in one of the ranch's pickups, with Bobby driving. He smelled distinctly of manure. Tied to the bumper, his mount followed along behind.

"Yep, I was one hell-raiser, ma'am." Bobby grinned almost proudly. "Into every chemical delight the world offered. The tedium of the textbook couldn't win against the illusions of the mind. My family disowned me. I dropped out of State, and when I couldn't afford the mind-benders, I began to steal."

She could empathize with the terrible loss of being disowned by one's family. "Is that how you ended up here, at Mescalero?"

"Yep. The judge was lenient on me. The big boss—"

"The big boss?"

"Tom."

"Of course," she said dryly. "That big boss."

"He's not lenient, but he keeps me too tired to think of anything besides a cold beer at the end of the day. That must be why I stay. He keeps me out of trouble. And you, ma'am." He flashed her a wicked grin. "You're not hard on the eyes, I'll say that for a fact."

Bobby amused her; she had to admit it. She wondered if one day he would care enough to replace those missing teeth. Probably only if he found it in himself to leave the security of the ranch for the outside world.

Water from the melted snow was running in every draw and every wrinkle in the land that afternoon. Overhead, the geese veed across the clear blue on their northward flight. Marianna took the driver's seat while Bobby mounted up—on a round-rumped mule, no less. Bobby had patiently explained what she was to do—block any dry cows, those that weren't expected to calve that year, from straying from the herd he was driving toward the east gate.

But her task wasn't as easy as he had made it sound. The bellowing cows were frisky with spring fever, and they exhibited something akin to intelligence. One walleyed cow paused for a drink of water, waited until Marianna's attention was diverted, then ran like hell. Off went Bobby, swearing and waving his hat and finally corralling it again. Another cow acted absorbed in grazing, then, as soon as it got the chance, ducked down into a gulch. Some just refused to move. They would lie down, look philosophical and chew their cuds with an expression that reminded Marianna of a wine taster savoring a special vintage.

Ugly bovines!

At last they were herded into the government-lease pasture, and a sweating Bobby took over driving back to the ranch house, regaling her with tales of Mescalero as he drove. "Yep, old Emmitt's been around here for a good many years. I hear that when he gets tired of the scenery he packs his possessions in his pickup and horse trailer and moves on to another ranch. But he always comes back."

She grudgingly admired the stubborn, independent quality of the everyday cowboy—a common laborer with heroic tendencies and a sense of humor.

Bobby also told her about the Malcolms themselves. "Yep, Red Eye claims that they were renegade rustlers a hundred years back. Running cattle over the border both ways. The old Indian says the Malcolms probably even have some Mexican blood in them."

"More like Attila the Hun's blood, I'd imagine," she observed dryly.

Since hazing the cows had taken longer than usual, it was late afternoon by the time they drove into the yard. Marianna fully expected some unpleasant remark from Tom. He always managed to find fault with her. Perhaps that was why she headed for her quarters first to clean up. She could never quite anticipate what he would say, so the best thing to do was just to stay out of his way as much as possible.

Shyloh, already home from school, was doing just the opposite. She was intent on watching Tom rope one of the heavy cows in the corral. The cow was stuck in the bog of melted snow and resisting all efforts. Marianna paused in the shadows of the machine shed to observe the process. Colt had a double-handed grip on the animal's tail, while Tom pulled with a rope. He wore only boots, jeans and a T-shirt, and his biceps were knotting and the muscles in his shoulders bulging with the effort. Perversity made her wish he would fall headfirst in the mud, but instead he safely dislodged the cow.

Shyloh must have asked a question, because he hunkered down to her level and began showing her something with the rope. Fascinated, Marianna watched as he swung a loop, increasing the size of his noose as the loop whirled. Peeved that the man might have any redeeming qualities, such as patience with a child, her child, Marianna swung away and continued toward the bunkhouse.

A fit of coughing warned her that Rob was inside. Warily she opened the screen door and followed the hacking sound to her bedroom. Rob stood there, holding up Marianna's black satin negligee. She draped the silky garment against herself and turned first this way, then that, watching the slinky material swirl. An almost enraptured expression softened the normally severe lines of the young woman's face.

"Like it?" Marianna asked.

Rob spun around. At the sight of Marianna's unsmiling countenance, her own blanched. "I was just...just..."

"Handling *my* clothes."

Marianna couldn't have dreamed up a more awkward situation in which to place the young woman, whose embarrassment was followed by a feeble attempt at justifying her actions. "You're late starting supper. I came to find you. This was lying on the bed, and I thought—"

The ends of Marianna's lips curved in an arch smile. "That you might look nice dressed as a woman after all."

Marianna had struck at the young woman's most vulnerable spot—her pride—and had made an implacable enemy. Rob exploded with anger. She threw the expensive nightgown on the floor and hissed, "Cheap floozy stuff. Get out! Get up to the house and make dinner!"

Marianna wisely didn't point out that this was her bedroom or that she had every right to change clothes before going back to work. After all, the Malcolms owned the place.

Owned *her*, or at least her services, when all was said and done.

Rob's humiliation must have cut deep, or else she was sicker than Marianna had imagined, because the young woman took to her bed, pleading illness, and didn't show up for dinner that evening. By the time Marianna finished washing the dishes, it was almost nine. On her way back to her quarters she skirted the grandstand, because that was where Tom usually lingered after dinner. She didn't glimpse the telltale glow of his cigar, but then, most times it wasn't lighted anyway.

She was far too aware of the man. Was it merely the lure of spring—the bulls rutting, the horses mating—that made her skin tingle, her breath come short, whenever he was near?

The heavens were a dense black, and she paused to watch a meteor shower. Even though the evening was cool, the meteors almost seemed to sear her with their greenish light. It was as if tension filled the air; even Rob's horses whinnied and galloped along the far fence. At that moment the moon appeared, an enormous pumpkin on the horizon.

Behind her, a voice said, "A wolf moon—an orange moon rising late."

She whirled. Tom stood there, hands in his back pockets, the cigar clamped in his teeth. Grooves of exhaustion ran from his nose to his mouth, and his eyes were heavy-lidded.

Her breath raced, and liquid shivers coursed the length of her body. "You startled me," she said, her voice unusually husky.

His eyes dropped to her softly parted lips. "I was out checking on a heifer that's sure to have a difficult birthing."

She nodded, uncertain what to reply, and started past him.

"Mind fixing a fresh pot of coffee?" His voice was deep, gentle. Out of keeping with his rough, tough looks, she thought. "I'm going to be making midnight and 2:00 a.m. checks, too," he explained.

She nodded again, but this time managed an "All right." She turned back to the ranch house, and he fell into step beside her. She slanted a glance at him. The moon was an alchemist, she thought, gilding his sun-streaked hair and mutating its gray to quicksilver.

He caught her stare. "Just what's on your mind?"

"Oh, just thinking about the moonlight," she hedged.

"What about it?"

He was going to make it difficult for her, she could see. "About how people sometimes say the moonlight is as bright as day. But I don't think so. It's a soft and caressing light, not a merciless and revealing one."

He opened the kitchen door for her. "I didn't reckon you were the type to find beauty in nature."

"You don't know anything about me," she retorted.

He took a seat at the table, tilting his chair back on its rear legs. "Then tell me."

His glinting gaze made her nervous. The heavy sexuality that had pervaded the air outside had seeped into the kitchen with them. She filled a coffeepot with water and measured out six heaping tablespoons of ground coffee. "What do you want to know?"

"Why didn't your parents testify on your behalf?"

The coffee grounds spilled onto the counter. She shot him a blistering glance. "You seem to know quite a lot about me already."

He shrugged. "The trial was in all the newspapers. Hard to miss."

She turned her back on him and set the pot on the stove. "They're living in Austria at the present. He's First Secretary at the embassy there."

"Airfare's not that expensive," he drawled.

She turned to face him, feeling perilously close to tears. Her mind clamped down on the pain of old memories. "All right. You want the truth? You've got it. They washed their hands of me when I got pregnant. Out of wedlock."

His gaze flickered to her face. "Jax Viking's child?"

So he'd heard of Jax. But then, anyone who watched television or read the newspapers had. "Yes."

Unconsciously she began pacing in front of the stove. "Mom and Dad loathed it when I began acting. It wasn't a legitimate career. Not the kind a diplomat's daughter should pursue. You have to know them. Very, very proper. After I became pregnant...it didn't matter that I had agreed to marry Jax. In their estimation he was nothing but a two-bit hard rock musician.

"When I went into labor...Mom wouldn't come to the hospital, even though she and Dad were barely three hours away by plane at the time, in D.C. My conviction last month merely justified their opinion of how far down the movie business had pulled me."

From upstairs came the staccato sound of Rob's coughing. Marianna glanced back at Tom. His dark face was set in hard, condemning lines. "When the coffee's ready," she snapped, "I'm sure you can pour it yourself."

Furious with herself for revealing her pain to him, she stalked out of the kitchen, letting the door slam behind her.

She couldn't sleep. The conversation with Tom had revived bitter recollections. Even during the trial, she hadn't let herself think about her parents' absence. In her mind, the tie had been severed years before, at Shyloh's birth. It was their loss, not hers. Still, she had felt so deserted, so alone, on that witness stand. Some of her friends had even abandoned her. Now that the pendulum of public opinion was swinging back toward an almost puritan morality, no one in the film industry could afford that kind of notoriety.

Trent was one of those friends who had stuck by her, and for that she felt a deep gratitude. Trent would have preferred something more—her love, most likely—but after Jax, she didn't think that love would ever touch her heart again.

At least not that kind of love. Her love for her daughter was another thing. Abiding, selfless, protective—that love brought out the best in her.

She padded barefoot down the hall to take a look at her sleeping daughter. Moonlight dusted Shyloh's hair. She was curled up, her thumb stuck in her mouth, a habit that had survived the toddler stage and to which she now succumbed only in her sleep. Marianna supposed that her dependence was the result of insecurity.

Old guilt assailed Marianna, guilt over the fact that she hadn't been the perfect mother, try as she had.

Whenever these guilt attacks occurred, she would remind herself that a perfect mother would be a walking catastrophe to the child. It didn't stop the occasional guilt attacks, though.

She returned to her own bedroom, but as she folded back the bedcovers she happened to glance out the window and see the light on in the barn. She checked her alarm clock. 2:35. The heifer Tom was worried about must be calving. There was a sense of rightness about the birthing process, and she regretted that she would probably never know that special kind of miracle again. Nature called out to her to come share the experience. She wrapped her terry-cloth robe around her, stepped into her slippers and stepped out of the bunkhouse.

The moon, silver now, hung low in the west. The sparse, tawny grass was wet from the dew. It had been so long since she had walked barefoot in dew-wet grass. Since childhood. How she wished she could do it now!

She found Tom in the big stall in back. He still wore the T-shirt, but it was blood-streaked, as were his tautly muscled arms. Hunkered on one knee, he stroked a heifer stretched out on the straw and spoke in a low, encouraging voice as he looped a lariat around the cow's neck. "All right, darlin', you can do it. You've done it before. I'm just here to help if you need me."

"Does it really help? The talking?"

His head jerked toward where she stood behind the stall gate. A smile that hinted at embarrassment eased the harsh lines of his mouth. "Don't you remember?"

"Jax wasn't there. Just a busy nurse."

"I see." He released her from his scrutiny and turned his attention back to the heaving cow. "I don't know that my voice actually calms the old girl. I guess I just want to let her know I'll stop hurting her as soon as I can." He rose to his full height and crossed to open the stall door for her. "How about giving me some help?"

She followed him back to the prone heifer, which bawled plaintively as it strained to expel the calf. "I don't know anything about delivering calves. I could talk to her, I suppose."

"I don't feel any more foolish talking with a cow," he said, "than I would to the average politician."

She smiled. At this time of night, or morning, the big boss didn't seem so formidable. Or perhaps it was the delicate task in which he was engaged that gentled his usually abrupt manner. "Is the cow in any real danger?"

"The calf may be too large in the shoulders. This heifer was bred to the Charolais. She should be large enough, she's an Amerifax—"

"Sounds like an airline."

He wrapped the lariat twice around a post. "It would take a cockpit computer to figure out the crossbreeding. Here, hold this end in case she throws her head. But if she starts to choke, turn her loose."

She watched as he dipped his hands and arms in a bucket of water that smelled as if it were mixed with some kind of antiseptic. "I'm going to pull the calf."

She did as he instructed while he inserted one arm into the birth canal, reaching into another cosmos. Birth. The cow's eyes were glazed from exhaustion, and it lay inert while Tom worked at repositioning the calf. "Mother Nature needs some help every now and then," he grunted.

Marianna felt tears come to her eyes as the cow, white eyes rolling, bellowed in pain. For almost thirty minutes Tom and Marianna worked together: he struggling to turn the calf and she, braced with the rope, talking in gentle tones to the worn-out mother cow.

All at once the calf slid out, all wet and matted with afterbirth. Tom reached for a gunnysack draped over the stall and tossed it to her. "Clean the little fella while I get Mama here on her feet."

Not quite sure what to do, she started with the calf's little face, wiping the sticky mucus from it. The calf gave a kind of gasp, shook its head and bawled weakly. Once it was clean, she saw that its face was white with curly hair. When she scratched behind its ears, it tried to lick her with its rough pink tongue. "How adorable," Marianna said, marveling at the harsh beauty of birthing.

"You haven't seen this end." Tom grinned. He was having trouble getting the cow to stand on its back legs. It was temporarily paralyzed from the birth, and its legs kept collapsing. At last it raised its head, nosed the calf and began to lick. When the calf nudged an udder and began to suckle, Tom sighed. "How about another pot of coffee? I'm bushed."

As they approached the house, the owl in the mesquite hooted twice, then spread its wings to catch the cool air of early morning. "Red Eye swears the owl keeps the evil eye away," Tom said.

Inside the kitchen, he pulled off his T-shirt while she washed her hands. Captivated, she watched as he took his turn at the faucet, lathering his arms and chest and face. The sight of his work-honed body—the tanned skin and rippling muscles and matted chest hair—began to stir sensations that had long been dormant. She turned quickly to the stove and began to take apart the coffeepot so she could brew more.

"It has to be satisfying whenever you've helped another life into the world," she murmured.

He toweled off. "And depressing as hell when you lose one." His hair was damp and curling at his temples, and he exuded a clean, soapy aroma.

"I've often thought I'd like another child, but—" She broke off, aghast at having admitted such a private thought.

"But what?" he asked.

He was standing too close to her as she filled the pot with water, and air was suddenly at a premium. They were staring at each other. She was captivated by the scarcely veiled danger of him, his strength, his strange, ethereal sensitivity. Time passed, measured only by the faint creaking of a house asleep.

She broke the spell, began measuring coffee into the pot. "But Jax was impatient with children."

"And?" he prodded.

She set the coffeepot on the stove. "Behind that tough rock-star image is a creative genius." She didn't know why she was telling Tom all this, babbling like a nervous teenager. "Jax's intelligence appealed to me. But his weaknesses didn't. He had to be the center of attention. He needed the idolatry—women, promoters, agents—to reassure him. You see, he didn't really know who he was. A child, even his own, was only in the way. When Shyloh was five, I divorced him."

Tom was watching her closely. His potent masculinity wrapped sensual streamers around her consciousness. "And there hasn't been anyone since?"

A heated blush suffused her skin, a deep, painful red that throbbed in her cheeks and temples. "That's none of your business."

He closed in on her. She had the overwhelming desire to twine her fingers through the hair that encircled his nipples. A maddening lust spiraled inside her, a whirling dervish of desire. She could only be thankful that he was repulsed by her kind of woman. That and that alone saved her from committing folly.

"Everything about you is my business," he said. "Remember?"

She forced her gaze to rise to his. "The coffee's ready," she murmured, then moved to pour him a cup.

He took a swallow. "Tastes terrible. Don't you know how to make a decent cup of coffee?"

The antagonism was back between them again. She felt like punching him. "No doubt remarks like that earned you your busted nose."

"Nope. The rodeo did that."

"Well, you can just make another pot yourself. I'm tired. Good night!"

Chapter 6

A wild passion flower.

Tom turned the shower on full force, sluicing the dust off a body sculpted to pure muscle by the nature of his work. Did Marianna have any idea what kind of flower she had set as a centerpiece on the breakfast table? A frivolous, feminine gesture.

Over the swollen, hot-blushed buds, he had watched her this morning. Spine royally straight, she had eaten with aristocratic motions, her hand daintily cupping the coffee mug, the little finger lifted imperiously. The others at the table, at least the men, had slanted glances at her with marveling eyes. The ranch hands seemed to blossom beneath the benevolent warmth of her million-kilowatt smile, just like the spring flower on the table.

Spring? There was no such thing in this quarter of New Mexico. After winter retreated, summer boiled up out of old Mexico, fierce and relentless.

Yet here I am, feeling like a randy goat in spring, he mocked himself.

Abruptly Tom adjusted the shower so that needles of cold water pelted down, only to be captured by the wiry hair matting his chest and furring the delta of his legs. Unfortunately, the icy shower didn't alter the direction of his thoughts.

I've had my season of passion. When love was fresh...when merely touching was sweet pain...yet never enough. When every thought was of...

He shut off the shower and stood with his feet planted apart, his hands braced against the wall. He rested his forehead against the wet tiles. Why not admit it? His every thought was of Marianna McKenna. A woman trained to project charm, to deceive the mind into thinking she was something she wasn't. Something she never could be.

His fists clenched. Remember, he told himself, Ruthie is real. Marianna is merely fantasy. Ruthie is solid strength. Dependable. Marianna is a will-o'-the-wisp.

Yet he was beguiled by Marianna. He would wake up in the middle of the night, his body bathed in sweat, her name...Marianna...Marianna...Marianna...a lyrical litany on his tongue.

He was too old for this kind of thing. He had a ranch he had to hang on to. He was only thirty-nine, but he felt a million years older. He had come to maturity in a different era, when peach-fuzzed American kids straight out of high school and college had come face-to-face with slant-eyed children bent on suicide missions.

When Western soldiers had been introduced to the delight of exotic Eastern drugs for the first time.

When a mine in a rice paddy could reduce a good buddy to a pulpy mass of flesh and bone.

When there had been no glory in fighting an undeclared war and coming home to scorn.

When your wife couldn't cope with a husband changed by that war.

Vivian had been his springtime.

And his winter.

She had been the governor's daughter, no less. A glamorous socialite, reminding him of a beautiful butterfly. They'd met in Santa Fe at a Sierra Club benefit rodeo. Because he'd been different from the businessmen she'd usually dated, she had been attracted to him. She had truly tried to be a rancher's wife, although she had hated every day of it, hated everything about it: the hot wind; the hot sun; the hot sand.

While he'd been away in Nam, something had changed. She'd quit trying, maybe. Or maybe it had been the money and good times flaunted by one of her father's associates, a wildcatter, that had dazzled her, turned her head.

The cutting words she had thrown at him when she had left—"You're nothing but a stupid, boring rancher!''—hadn't hurt, because he'd warned her from the beginning that he never intended to be anything but a rancher. But losing her... For a long while that pain had been as constant as his heartbeat.

With a grunt, he straightened and plowed a hand through his thick hair. Despite the shower, he felt far from refreshed. Discontent plagued him. After Vivian had moved back to Santa Fe with that wildcatter, Tom had felt...nothing. An emptiness, maybe. But most days the effort required by ranch work had kept him from feeling restless. In bed, Ruthie's unimaginative loving had kept him satisfied.

Until now.

Now he ached like a bull in rut.

Buck-naked, he padded across to the ancient armoire that had been his great-grandfather's and searched for a pair of briefs in one of the drawers Vivian had installed just after they had married. As he shrugged into clean jeans, he became aware of a rustling in the adjoining room, his office.

Red Eye, trying to remember where he might have hidden a liquor bottle? Always a hearty drinker, the old man had taken up drinking as a career after Grandmother Ella had died.

Bobby? Reverting to his old ways and looking for some easy money?

With a stealth left over from jungle combat duty, Tom moved toward the connecting doorway. Because of the blue handkerchief covering her hair and knotted at her nape, he thought at first the woman was Rob. In the next instant the softly rounded arms and cream-colored flesh betrayed the intruder's identity: Marianna. She was going through a desk drawer.

"Can I help you?" he drawled.

She spun around. Her startled gaze took in his bare chest and the triangular patch of his stomach revealed by his unzipped jeans. "You're back early." Her hands knocked a can of furniture polish off the desk.

He sauntered over to her and picked up the can, holding it out to her. "I asked if I could help you find what you were looking for."

"I was looking for... Rob sent me in here to find her telephone book. She said it'd be—"

"Rob doesn't have one."

"But she—" Marianna's eyes narrowed. "You don't believe me, do you? Why would I be snooping in your personal papers?"

He braced his hands on the desk edge, one on either side of her enticing hips. His nostrils flared, detecting the elusive scent of her perfume, which reminded him of honeysuckle and wildflowers and sweet grass. He could feel himself getting aroused without even touching her. "The drawer to your left contains the ranch's supply of petty cash. Enough to get someone to the border. It's kept locked."

Her mouth rounded in astonishment, then tightened into a thin line. "So that's what she was up—"

"What?"

"Nothing." Her teeth worried her lower lip. He stifled an overpowering urge to taste those lips, soft and unmarred by the harsh weather. "Now what happens?" she asked. "Do you send me back?"

Now what happens? I take you and kiss you again and again until that polite, disdainful smile dissolves. "Do you want to go back?"

"You know I don't."

"Because you enjoy being my prisoner?"

Her eyes snapped. "I could never enjoy that!"

"I think you could. I think I'm a better choice than seven years in jail."

She arched a haughty brow. "If you're insinuating that I should go to bed with you . . ."

He felt whirlpools of hot, sweet heaviness in his blood. "Who said anything about bed? And if I decided I wanted you in my bed, I certainly wouldn't bother insinuating anything—I'd take you there."

He straightened and stepped away, because the mere suggestion of what had been haunting his daylight hours and nightly dreams was drawing him perilously close to making it a reality. His track record with women was abysmal, and he would be a fool to think that the stereotype of femininity, this actress trained to simulate passion, knew anything about the real thing.

Her eyes flared. "You really are arrogant, aren't you?"

"Unless you want to do seven years of hard time," he said, his voice rough, "I'd suggest that you stay out of my desk."

For a moment she didn't move. A variety of emotions flickered over her countenance: rage, fear, curiosity. Then her expression quickly closed. "Tell me, why do you do this? Work with convicts?"

As good as he was at reading expressions, he was at a loss now, and he damned well didn't appreciate not being in control. "I'm weird, darlin'. I get my kicks helping people with drug problems."

"We all need help. Even yourself."

A heavy, dark feeling of old pain made him mute with rage at himself and at her. Where was his cowboy's stoicism? He jerked his head toward the hallway. "I imagine you have a houseful of furniture to finish polishing."

The utility room had a drier, but the weather that Saturday was already so warm that Marianna decided to hang out the freshly washed clothing. Behind the ranch house, a line had been strung between the patio's limestone wall and a nearby mesquite. Because Rob had been the only woman and had had to cook and clean house and rope cattle and break horses, the clothesline had seen little use. According to Red Eye, it was easier to toss the laundry into the drier.

Marianna, however, preferred to hang things out. She could have explained how much fresher the clothes smelled, and how much money was saved by hanging them on the line, but the simple truth was that she enjoyed the sunshine, the outdoors. No, it was more than that. She *needed* the sunshine and the outdoors. Those five days of internment had made an indelible impression on her psyche.

At first she hadn't realized how much imprisonment had affected her, but after being trapped in the pantry, she'd found that lately she was leaving the bedroom door open when she slept. She was also awakening quite often in the middle of the night to find the light still on. She had attributed it to falling asleep while reading. Thank God Shyloh's sleep was undisturbed by her mother's foolish nightmares.

She could hear Shyloh's childish laughter now. Colt had put her on the mechanical bull that Rob used to train her cutting horses.

"Marianna."

Marianna turned to find Rob standing in the doorway, holding open the screen door. A slight frown furrowed the younger woman's straight black brows.

Now what? Marianna wondered. After the way Rob had set her up, tricking her into going through Tom's desk, Marianna was extremely cautious. Tom's sister wanted her off Mescalero—the sooner the better—and she was prepared to go to almost any lengths to achieve that objective.

"Yes?" she asked wearily.

"You have a telephone call."

Nervous flutterings churned Marianna's stomach. The only person who knew she was here was her agent. And, of course, the authorities. Whoever it was, the call had to be important. Bad news or good? There had been so little good news over the past five months that she was conditioned by now to expect the worst.

She took the call in the privacy of Tom's office. Here, among books on horses and cattle—vet books, grooming books, pedigree books—her nostrils absorbed the scent of leather, his odious cigars and him. Something in her body quivered in a purely sensual reaction. Remembering the week before, when he had come upon her in this room, she felt the heat of excitement quiver between her legs. A vision of that wickedly muscular body tantalized her. It was dissolute to want to make love to a man whom she didn't even like. And she most certainly didn't like the direction her thoughts took when he was around.

She was accustomed to men trying not to look at her, hiding their bedroom appraisals of her under a veneer of sophistication. But Tom made no effort to hide his interest in her. Yet it was almost an indifferent interest. She interested him as if she were a Martian.

Despite that, whenever she was about to decide he was a grim, humorless man, he would grin and make some offhand remark—and she would catch herself smiling. Something about his quiet humor and earthy openness appealed to her. More than that, it excited her, though she had trained herself over the years never to betray emotions the movie industry, film critics and the news media could trample upon.

She picked up the receiver. "Hello?"

"Marianna? Trent here."

An image of his handsome, scholarly face came to mind as she asked, "Has something come up, Trent?"

"I'm afraid so. Your house in Mesilla was broken into last night."

"Oh, my God! Is Enriqueta all right?"

"It happened while she was away. She came back and found the signs of forced entry."

Of course. Enriqueta took the weekends off to visit her family. "Did she say what was stolen?"

"Apparently nothing. At least from what she can tell."

"I have an itemized list of my household goods in my safe deposit box, if that will help."

"Marianna, from what I can glean from talking with Enriqueta and the Mesilla police chief, the place looks like a bargain-basement sale the day after. Someone was obviously looking for something."

Marianna's eyes narrowed thoughtfully. "I don't keep anything especially valuable in the house."

"Well, I'll keep you informed of any developments. Are you all right? Is that Malcolm guy treating you well?"

"Yes, I'm fine, Trent." She had to smile. "And 'that Malcolm guy' is treating me fine." She supposed she could be forgiven for what was at least half a lie. "Now stop worrying. I've only got three months and three weeks to go." It felt like forever.

"You know I care?"

"Yes, I know you care," she repeated softly.

But she couldn't offer him the same assurance. Her marriage to Jax Viking—really Jack Voorheis—had been a disaster from the start. She had loved Jax wildly, fully and, yes, foolishly. Over the years in Hollywood she had come to learn that even the most astute businesswoman, the most sophisticated society matron, the most talented ingenue, could behave foolishly when it came to a man.

"Take care of yourself, honey," Trent said. "And watch out for that Malcolm guy. I worry about you, you know."

"I can handle myself with Malcolm and his kind. Bye," she finished softly.

Thoughtfully she replaced the telephone in the cradle and stared at it. When at last she looked up, Tom was watching her from the doorway. He was dressed in a clean pair of jeans and a white dress shirt, the sleeves rolled up on his forearms to reveal crisp brown hair.

How much had he heard?

His implacable, wolfish grin didn't disguise the menace in his voice. "Want to show me how?"

She licked her lips. "How what?"

He ambled over to her, halting only intimidating inches away from her. "How you handle big, plodding yokels like me."

A nervous spasm ticked in her throat. "I didn't say that. I meant—"

"Tom?"

Both Marianna and Tom turned toward the hallway door, where Ruthie stood, dressed in a flounced skirt and peasant blouse. She looked somehow out of place in the feminine attire. Her eyes glanced from Marianna to Tom, but Marianna couldn't tell just what Ruthie was thinking. She smiled amiably. "Just stopped by to drop off a gallon jar of honey I'd put up. What time you going over to the trading post?"

Tom gave Marianna a blistering glance, then turned his full attention to Ruthie. "We're on our way, soon as I round everyone up."

"You coming to the dance tonight, Miss McKenna?" she asked.

"Uh, no. I hadn't—"

Ruthie flicked her turquoise gaze to Tom. "Why not, Tom? Besides, Miss McKenna's daughter would really enjoy the outing." She glanced at Marianna. "I met your daughter outside. She's a delightful child."

Tom took Ruthie's elbow. "Ruthie, let me run my own business."

She glanced over her shoulder at Marianna. "See you this evening."

Nothing was more colorful than a Saturday-night dance at the Border Bluff Trading Post. Excitement, almost a vibration in the air, started forming early in the day. Cowhands began showering and spruсing up in the late afternoon. On the Mexican side of the border, the *señoritas* would put on their best finery and, accompanied by a cousin, uncle or duenna, make their way to the trading post.

An outrageously gorgeous sunset filled the western sky, both a single naked light bulb and hanging paper lanterns already lighted the enormous covered porch. It had been cleared of its pool table, and Mexican musicians were warming up two guitars, a violin and trumpet.

Come nightfall, the surrounding flat would be filled with cars, tethered horses, buckboards and pickups whose headlights would be switched on to light the way for the couples who could find no room to dance on the covered porch. When the musicians took a break, the automobile radios would be turned up full blast, and couples would surge between the parked vehicles to dance under the stars. Advantage had to be taken of every precious moment of these rare socials.

Marianna was dressed in a simple white cotton skirt and blouse from Rodeo Drive that would have cost a ranch hand a month's salary. She watched the festivities from one shadowy porch corner. Next to her, Shyloh stood in silent awe, her eyes wide, her mouth parted. For her, the social was better than any grand ball. Marianna had spent almost half an hour trying to brush Shyloh's unruly blond curls into soft, gilded waves, then finally abandoned her efforts as fruitless when Shyloh had begun to fuss and wiggle.

Together, mother and daughter observed the merrymaking. Revelers streamed out of the open door with cans of beer and soda they had bought inside. Others conversed in Spanish, English and Tex-Mex. The women talked about who had had babies and who had died. The men discussed wetter or drier years, and worse winters. Red Eye was corralled with several Hispanic vaqueros behind a pickup. Emmitt, rolling his chewing tobacco inside his lip, swapped tall stories with other ranch hands.

If the revelers weren't drinking or talking and laughing, they were dancing, mostly old-fashioned favorites at the moment, like the waltz, the polka, the schottische. To a Mexican version of "Cotton-eyed

Joe," a fat, middle-aged housewife in tight jeans and flip-flops paraded by with a good-looking cowhand of twenty or so. Two men danced together for lack of women. A grandfather danced with a toddler. Bobby propelled a hand mop for a partner. When he grew tired of that, he pinched the bottom of the old woman in front of him. She squealed with delight.

"Dance, *señorita*?" Rand asked, sweeping off his Stetson and bowing low before a suddenly bashful Shyloh. His eyes sparkled with merriment.

Shyloh glanced up at Marianna. "Can I, Mom?"

"Sure, babe."

Rand gallantly edged a path through the dancers for Shyloh. This was what Shyloh had needed all along, Marianna thought. Hollywood's life-style would have eaten her up.

It almost did me.

When Marianna lost sight of the two temporarily, her gaze slid over the others. Nearby, she found Tom's big silhouette. He was joking with a group of ranchers and their wives. The homesteaders were as cliquish as film people. And their conversations all centered around the land.

"...cattle got sour and wouldn't honor a horse..."

"I was so dry I had to sell. Weren't enough grass on me to feed a jackrabbit."

She thought how appropriate their choice of words was. They *were* the land.

Ruthie was with them. Her arm lay across the back of Tom's waist but reached no further. The man was too massive. Big men had always intimidated Mar-

ianna, though she wasn't sure why, exactly. Tom
Malcolm intimidated her most of all, and in his case
she knew exactly why. He held over her what
amounted to the power of life and death.

Then, too, he affected her in another way. Forbidden images of his muscular body heavy on hers, his
powerful hand between her thighs, sent waves of heat
through her. Quickly she averted her eyes. What was
wrong with her? She had never been given to sexual
fantasies before.

Disgusted with her errant thoughts, she forced her
attention back to the dance floor. All but three people on the porch were dancing, she noted. Colt
watched with opaque, Indian-black eyes. Since the
fourteen-year-old was neither Anglo nor Hispanic, he
was relegated to the netherworld, ostracized.

Marianna's gaze moved on to Rob. The girl was
smiling easily, but Marianna didn't miss the scorn in
her eyes. As scarce as women were here, no man had
the courage to approach Rob.

And then, thought Marianna, there's me. She
caught the curious glances cast her way, the whispered "...actress...movie star..." The fact that she
was also a convict made little difference. The people
who had settled here generations before had themselves been on the run from the long arm of the law—
horse thieves, gamblers, cattle rustlers, ladies of the
night. No, it was her glamorous, aloof image that kept
her a wallflower. Even Bobby flirted but didn't dare
ask.

There was another who didn't dance, but he had just arrived. Like Tom and the other cattlemen, he wore jeans and a dress shirt with a black string tie. But beneath the flap of his casual jacket she could see a pistol. With surprise, she watched him approach her.

"Howdy, ma'am," he said, tipping his hat.

His clothes couldn't hide the fact that he was running to fat. He had thinning hair and steely, ball-bearing eyes that were a little too watchful. Uncertain, she said only, "Hello."

"Reese," he said. "Cal Reese, County Sheriff."

Her heart tripped over its own beat. Had he been sent to bring her back to prison? She was terrified, but would rather have died than show it. She forced herself to eye him coolly and wait for an explanation.

"Heard you're Malcolm's latest convict," he went on in a friendly way. "Just wanted to check you out. You got any problems, you come to me, hear?"

"She'll come to *me*, Reese."

She looked beyond the county sheriff to Tom. He took her arm. "Excuse us," he told Reese curtly, then propelled her across the dance floor.

"What was that all about?" she asked as he drew her through the crowd.

"Just shut up," he rumbled. "The Feds had to send a woman," he muttered. "As if I didn't have trouble enough trying to keep the ranch going."

Why did he have to keep throwing her conviction in her face? "Oh, don't worry. I know my place. Shouldn't I be walking behind you instead of alongside? My head should be bowed meekly, shouldn't it,

Mr. Malcolm? I know you wouldn't want anyone to know you had allowed your prisoner any extra privileges."

She had the satisfaction of seeing him scowl down at her. "Lady, that three months and three weeks can't pass any more quickly for you than they can for me!"

He opened the door to his pickup and thrust her inside. "Just stay put. I'll be back with Shyloh in a moment."

Lips tight, she watched him wend his way back through the crowd. He was cruel to cut the evening short like this. Shyloh had been having such a good time. What had angered him? Jealousy? Surely not of that sheriff.

"You go?"

Startled, she jumped. Red Eye stuck his head through the open pickup window. "Tom says so," she muttered.

"Damn fine shame. Everyone have one hot-damn time."

"So was I, until Tom dragged me away from Cal Reese." The old Indian's eyes widened, and she realized just how red they really were. "You've been drinking, Red Eye."

He held up a brown bottle and grinned. "Sotol. Good for tired ying-yang."

She rolled her eyes. "I don't think I'd better ask what ying-yang is."

"County sheriff only wants to cause hot-damn trouble. He wants convict program to go. He wants Mescalero on auction table."

"Auction block?"

"You betcha. Part of Mescalero was his and his brother Doyle's. Then Tom bought it."

"I see." That explained why Tom had gotten her out of there so rapidly. If Cal Reese found any misconduct going on, especially of a sexual nature, that would shut Mescalero down quickly enough. Just one more reason for Tom to want her off Mescalero. She spotted Tom with Shyloh. He had stopped to say something to Ruthie.

"I don't understand how any woman puts up with that man," Marianna mumbled.

"Only woman fit for Tom will be woman with heart, brain and sand."

She supposed that "sand" was his term for grit. Hmmph!

"Want some sotol?" he asked cheerfully.

"Don't tempt me."

Chapter 7

Marianna laid Rand's T-shirt atop his pile of folded clothes. The *azulejo*, or tiled, counter, which ran the length of the utility room, was covered with the mounds of clothes she had folded. Built hotelstyle to service the Malcolms, as well as Mescalero's numerous ranch hands, the utility room had seen reduced service in the last few years. The linoleum floor was corroded by the washing machine's spillover, and the counter was chipped in spots.

She picked up a pair of Tom's white briefs, and her hands lingered as she folded the cotton underwear. Impulsively she rubbed the clean, line-dried briefs against her cheek. They smelled of soap and sunshine and heat—the way he did.

What was wrong with her? Why this preoccupation

with that rough-edged cowboy? Had her abstinence of the last few years left her obsessed with sex?

No, she knew that wasn't it. She wasn't panting to go to bed with Bobby, who would love the opportunity. Or anyone else, for that matter. Her marriage had been a destructive one, a brutal emotional struggle. After she and Jax had divorced she had gone through a year of frantic dating—an effort, she supposed, to prove that she was still worthy as a woman. Those dates had invariably culminated in juvenile groping that left her empty and with a bad taste in her mouth. As a result, she had buried herself in her work for the past three or four years, keeping so busy that she hadn't even thought about sex.

Until recently.

"Get the bedroom door, Rand!"

At the sound of Tom's urgent voice, she dropped the briefs and hurried to the doorway just in time to see him carrying Rob down the hall in his arms. As big as the young woman was, he maneuvered her easily. The big rowels on his high-heeled boots rang like bells.

Marianna followed them into the young woman's bedroom. There were so many unused bedrooms, lovely rooms with Victorian-era wallpaper, to pick from, yet Tom's sister had selected this sparsely furnished cubicle, which looked more like a nun's cell.

Rob was stretched out on the bed, her eyes closed. As Tom ran his hands over first one arm and then the other, her teeth bit into her lower lip.

Tom's thick brows lowered. "Fractured. Both of them. Near the wrist joint."

"I should've known better than to ride that damn filly. Not when she's just green broke."

"You should've known better than to try and break the fall with your arms thrust out like that and your hands bent backward. Rand, go out to the barn and make two splints out of that plywood in the back of the tack room—a forearm's length."

"Ouch!" Rob gritted out. "Tom, I'm not a steer you're wrestling."

"Can I help?" Marianna asked.

He glanced over his shoulder. His expression told her that he didn't think she would ever be much help for anything. "Get two old towels for padding."

She nodded and started out the door. The tears she blinked back had to come from frustration. Didn't they?

Emmitt eyed his dinner sourly, his mouth compressed into a tight line. He blinked several times, and Marianna knew that he was getting ready to speak—or grumble, as the case usually was. "What is it?" he finally asked.

Her hands on her lips, she eyed the stringy man narrowly. But it was Shyloh who piped up in a cheerful voice, "Swedish meatballs, Emmitt. They're good."

"Some kind of foreign dish?" Rand asked.

Marianna expelled a disgusted breath. "It's time all you hombres learned that hamburger doesn't always have to come in a round pattycake."

Living in the various countries where her father had been posted, she had come to appreciate international cuisine. Since her parents had often had to give dinners for visiting dignitaries, she had learned that some of the European masterpieces were much simpler to cook than they sounded. She was willing to wager her next role that before she left Mescalero, she would have the men eating veal scaloppine, chicken cacciatore and beef Stroganoff—and loving every mouthful!

"Dig in, men," Tom ordered. "This can't be any worse than the tortillas."

There he went, goading her again. She was tired of his hammering away at her defenses. Her only asset on the ranch was a stiff upper lip. She had to take whatever was dished out and keep on going. But not this time. "Tom Malcolm," she said sweetly, "you're a male-chauvinist sexist hypocritical bigot!"

He did a double take. The men around him tried to suppress their smirks.

"Meat's better 'n buffalo," Red Eye said.

"You ate buffalo?" Shyloh asked him, her eyes wide. "Real buffalo?"

Deciding that discretion was indeed the better part of valor, Marianna left Shyloh to entertain the men, who, she noted, were eating quite heartily. Rob still had to be dealt with. Marianna prepared a dinner tray and took it to Rob, who was pacing her bedroom like a wild mustang that had just been corralled.

"Shouldn't you be resting?"

"What good's resting going to do for two fractured wrists?" Rob demanded testily.

"Maybe none, but that analgesic you took would get better results if you tried to relax."

"Can't do a thing all wrapped up like a mummy." Her face sullen, she held up both arms, stiff with the new casts the doctor had put on.

Marianna managed a smile and set the tray on the nightstand. "Oh, I'm sure there are some things you can do around the house here. Things that don't require a lot of exertion."

Rob turned on her, angry tears sparkling in her eyes. Her gaze swept a blistering path over Marianna's pale lavender sundress. "Like what? I'm not a hothouse flower like you! All I know how to do is work."

"Then it's time you learned how to enjoy the art of resting," Marianna replied impatiently, all the while thinking that the girl's words had revealed more about her than she would have cared to have anyone know. "Come and sit down, Rob. I'll feed you until you get accustomed to your casts."

"I don't need a baby-sitter!"

Marianna shrugged. "All right. Call me if you change your mind."

But of course Rob would never admit to needing help. Just like her brother. The Malcolms were too arrogant for their own good. Especially Tom.

As Marianna returned to the dining room, she could hear his voice. "...puts us in a hell of a predicament. A pen of cattle to work, calves to be branded and castrated—"

"The Slaughter Mesa windmill needs repairing," Colt added in that laconic, velvet-soft tone. "Not a lick of water there."

Emmitt nodded as Marianna entered. "Bad time for Rob to give out."

Marianna surveyed the men; deep concern was etched on their faces, though their voices were mild enough. "I can help out."

All heads turned toward her. Every man gaped except Tom. He appraised her slowly, from her slender ankles to her delicate forearms. Then his eyes met hers, and she saw the open derision glittering there. "Oh, really? Want to tell me your own special technique for castrating a calf?"

She planted her fists on her hips and made sure each man at the table noted her disgust. "I've never been on a working ranch, only those resorts you all scorn so. But I *can* ride."

"How well?"

"Well enough. When my family lived in France, my father would take me horseback riding on the beach in Deauville, or at Chantilly, near Paris."

"Pleasure riding!" he scoffed.

"Look, if you want my help, fine. If not, then just sit there and groan and gripe about all the work that's not going to get done."

"Well, now, Miss McKenna," he growled, "I think I'll call your bluff. Be ready to saddle up first thing tomorrow morning." He turned to Shyloh. "Can you help Red Eye take care of Rob for the next few days?"

"You betcha!" she said.

Why was it that the man's ferocious snarl which was supposed to pass for a smile but didn't fool her for a minute, left Shyloh unfazed?

On the one hand, the Mescalero cowboys wanted to show their best side; on the other, they didn't care if anyone was there to see it or not.

Marianna tried to do what she was told and stay out of the way. She had met a few drugstore cowboys, mostly stuntmen or wranglers in the movie industry—men who were a lot more show than substance—but she was finding that the Mescalero bunch were long on substance.

The first day, Saturday, she rode with Rand, who took a not-so-subtle pride in demonstrating his knowledge. "Yup, Miss McKenna, all the cowboys' clothes come from the conquistadores." He pointed to her spurs. "The ones with rowels are sometimes called *nazarenos*, 'cause they look like the crown of thorns."

They rode across a barren brown plateau thicketed with scrub brush and crisscrossed by gullies and foothills. From that point, Mescalero stretched almost fifty-five miles to the north. Even Rand didn't know the exact size of the ranch.

"...but in a good year Mescalero's grazing capacity is somewhere 'tween five to six thousand cows with calves or eleven to twelve thousand heifers and bulls."

She and Rand were moving sixty-five head of cattle from the cinnabar section to a summer pasture that was known as the Cimarron Draw. As far as she was concerned, there wasn't enough grass on the desolate landscape to feed a stringy jackrabbit, but the cattle looked healthy enough. D.O.G. followed along, dashing here and there to mark the territory as his.

The days were longer now. The sage had begun to turn green, and the wild plum were bursting into flower. The cottonwood trees sent out their buds, and blooming yucca filled the rocky draws. On such a day, Marianna could almost understand why a man preferred the cowboy way of life.

Almost.

Because by midmorning the May sunlight was glaring down like a laser beam. There wasn't even a suggestion of a breeze over the white stretch of desert. The cows moved slowly, panting in the heat, and the calves walked with their heads drooping and foam between their lips. Their hooves kicked up little puffs of dust.

She was glad now that Tom had insisted on her wearing one of Rob's hats, a shapeless old thing, or else her brain would have been fricasseed. Colt had donated a pair of boots that were too small for him. They were a good five years old, at least, but they came close to fitting her small feet. Shotgun chaps completed her outfit.

"Holistic ranch management is what Dad calls it," Rand was saying. "It's a complicated rotation plan. Dad had the New Mexico State University agriculture extension service figure out the plan. It's more work, 'cause you have to move the cattle about every three months. See, the action of their hooves actually increases the land's fertility. That sure as hell—excuse me, ma'am—sure surprised some of them environmentalists."

She removed her hat to fan her face. What she wouldn't give right now for a fruit jar of iced tea, the moisture streaming down the glass. Oh, to wade in a cold, high mountain steam at that moment! The mare she rode, a steel-mouthed bay, was already steaming at the flanks, and it wasn't even noon yet. "Sounds like you're planning on following in your father's footsteps."

"You bet. Wouldn't ever want to do anything else." He grinned sideways at her. "Nothing like being your own man. Taking pride in the quality and condition of the cattle you've raised. It's downright satisfying to get up at dawn and ride out to check your cows, see which one has calved in the night."

She started to tell him that she hadn't recalled seeing him in the barn before dawn, helping a cow to calve. Instead, she let her curiosity have its way. "Your mom, is she from this area?"

"Oh, no. She's a city woman, like yourself, Miss McKenna. Born and raised in Santa Fe. Met Dad at a benefit rodeo up there. My granddad was governor of the state at one time."

"Do you see her very often?"

"When she and Dad divorced—I was five—I went to live with her in Santa Fe. While I was there, my allergies exploded, and so did Mom's patience, so I came back. I see her and my grandparents at Christmas and Easter, and that's about it.''

"And Colt?" she asked casually. "Is he your stepbrother?"

"Half brother." He unknotted the red handkerchief from around his neck and mopped his face. "Colt's mom was a Whitetail Apache off the Mescalero Indian Reservation."

"Was?"

"She died of a drug overdose."

Unlike many of the modern outfits, Mescalero hadn't switched to the calf cradle, or working chute, for branding the calves born during the winter. Tom still used the old-fashioned roping method.

Watching Tom ride his buckskin into the herd was like catching a glimpse of the legacy of the Old West. Like watching a legend in the making. He must have been born with chaps on. Marianna saw it in the way he and all the Mescalero cowboys did their jobs.

Sitting astride his horse, he moved with ease and grace, exuding confidence and quiet authority. He roped each calf by the hind feet, took his dally, a slack noose, and dragged it in. Then Rand and Bobby threw the calf to the ground, and Emmitt brought the iron and did the actual branding. The iron had been heated red-hot by a propane fire, and a cloud of acrid yellow smoke billowed off each calf's seared hide as the mark of the Double M was branded on its right side.

Marianna pressed her lips tightly together to fight back her objections.

"Cattle are tough, ma'am," Rand said, "and calves don't anticipate pain like a human will."

"Tell that to the calf," she muttered. But the branded calves, released, shot up like champagne corks, apparently none the worse for the ordeal.

Twice Bobby got his arm burned by the hot iron, and a kicking calf mashed Rand's finger. No one escaped unbruised, and everyone was hot and sweating from the nearby fire and the hot sun, covered with dirt and blood and coughing from the dust and smoke.

"Let's take off and go into town for a beer," Bobby suggested.

No one bothered to answer.

Colt stood next to her, waiting as she was for the next calf. They were working as a team today. Once a calf with the Mescalero-Malcolm double M, was branded, Colt used a vaccine gun to inoculate it against black leg. Then she did her bit, trying to clamp off any small, budding horns with a mechanical clipper. She tried not to show her squeamishness when blood occasionally spurted. Once she caught Tom's hard-edged gaze on her, but she couldn't tell whether it was filled with approval or impatience.

When Rand castrated the first male calf, she was unable to control a shiver. "You can't tell me that doesn't hurt," she said.

He grinned. "Can't say. I've never been castrated."

"You've never been branded, either," she said grimly.

She tried not to cringe when he repeated the process with the next calf, but the bawling and the bleeding were more than she could take. Or maybe it was just the heat. The high-necked, long-sleeved blouse she had worn to protect herself against the burning sun seemed to choke her. The sky started to spin, and the vulture circling overhead whirled faster and faster. She felt as if she were on one of the rotating gyro rides at the state fair.

"Are you all right, ma'am?" It was Colt's voice, but it was coming from so far away.

"I think . . ." Then someone was catching her, carrying her.

In the distance she heard someone else—Emmitt, maybe—say, ". . . limp as a half sack of grain."

She felt the ground beneath her, something metal bracing her back, then a wet cloth pressed against her forehead and at her throat. She opened her eyes. She was propped against the tank of the windmill. Tom was kneeling over her, his chiseled features taut as he bathed her with his dampened red flannel handkerchief. His green-flecked stare rose from her throat to her face.

"You look like hell," he told her.

She dragged her gaze from the hard, sensuous line of his mouth. The ignominy of fainting! She struggled to rise, but he pushed her back against the tank.

"Don't get up too quickly," he warned.

Her hand went to her throat. Only then did she realize that her blouse was gaping, exposing the creamy swells of her breasts. Her fingers fumbled with the top buttons before she realized they had been torn away.

He reached down and plucked some kind of fern. She felt the full impact of his narrow, glittering gaze as he bent his head to her. Then he began rubbing the fern first behind her ear at a pulse point and next at her throat, where her blood pounded wildly. His hand paused there, and her nerves began jangling at his touch. For several searing seconds they stared at each other. A remorselessly sexual heat burned through her.

"Spearmint," he growled. "It'll revive you quickly enough."

She could feel that stare, as sharp as a knife against her throat. "I'm all right. Really."

"Let's break for lunch," he called over his shoulder, and stood up.

She rose on her own, declining his proffered hand, and followed the crew back to the house. At the table, Shyloh's glowing eyes betrayed her pride at helping with the meal. "I made the potato salad, Mom—and the iced tea!"

"That's wonderful, babe," Marianna managed to say. She still felt shaky.

No one mentioned her fainting. They talked of the branding...how many calves were left...if a new tool should be used in place of the knife...the silver moon last night with the ring around it, which was supposed to indicate a change in weather.

But she saw the pity in their eyes. How galling!

After lunch everyone adjourned to the veranda, where it was cooler. Colt sat on a cedar railing, his back braced against a post, and strummed a Spanish guitar. Shyloh's eyes glowed with adulation as she listened along with the rest of the Mescalero crew while he sang an old cowboy song. Everyone, even old Red Eye, joined in for the chorus—everyone except Tom.

Marianna sat in the veranda swing with Bobby, but her eyes kept straying to the steps, where Tom sat. The heat she felt for him still beat in her veins. She tried to tell herself that he was just another man, but in his boots, Stetson, vest and chaps, he looked anything but ordinary. In fact, he made the Marlboro Man look like Mickey Mouse, she decided. She was tempted to say he was handsome, even though he lacked the physical perfection that Hollywood usually associated with that term.

His unlighted cigar was clamped between his strong white teeth, and his eyes had a far-off glaze. Did he regret being a cowboy? She doubted it. Rand had told her that his father had finished his schooling on the GI Bill at night, commuting to NMSU. Perhaps that education was something to fall back on, but for men like Tom, she suspected, there was no other life but this one.

Not so for her. She hated the extremes—the heat, the cold, the eternal winds and endless sand. She hated the hard physical labor—and Tom's relentless demands on her.

The moon was huge, with a ring around it again. What kind of moon would Tom call it? And why this crazed obsession with him? Why did she seek his tough-minded love?

Even now, her footsteps took her toward the grandstand, though she knew he wouldn't be there. He was avoiding her, as she should him. Had she no pride?

She halted at a mesquite tree and lighted a cigarette. She felt its soothing smoke eddy through her lungs, easing her jangled nerves. The day had been a rough one. She was bone-tired. And humiliated. And sunburned. So much for her fair skin. If she stayed at the ranch long enough, she would look like some freckle-faced kid, with a bad case of chicken pox, to boot.

Thank God she had less than three months remaining! Because much longer than that and she'd end up making a real fool of herself.

Restless, she tossed the cigarette on the ground and ground it out with her boot. She pushed the tangled curtain of her hair back off her neck and splayed the strands with her fingers. The night was hot. The large, darkened house seemed like a ship, sitting motionless on a sea of desert sand, hoping for a breeze to fill its sails.

She leaned against the mesquite, feeling its rough bark through her blouse. It seemed she could almost sense the heat drumming under the tree's bark, like the earth's heartbeat. Like the need drumming in her blood. A hard, hurting knot in her body.

She straightened away from the tree, her skin prickling. There was something there in the dark.

Watching. Her hand went to her throat, and her flesh felt cold.

"Who's there?" she asked.

Only silence.

She edged around the tree, starting back toward her bunkhouse—and almost shrieked. There, lying dead in the dirt, was the owl. "Oh, no!" she whispered.

Carefully she picked it up, marveling at its softness, at the thickness of its feathers. No telling what had caused it to die. Heat. Old age. Disease. She thought about burying it, but somehow that seemed like a desecration—an eternal end to the bird's wild, free flight. Instead, she lifted it and, stretching, nestled it into a high crevice of the mesquite. Nature, the sun and rain and wind, would administer its funeral rites.

She felt as if unseen eyes still followed her when she at last returned to her quarters, but she was no longer afraid.

Only lonely.

And wanting. Yearning. Longing.

Chapter 8

Good God, pay attention, will you? The pliers, not the file. Hand me the pliers!''

Marianna closed her eyes. The dizziness didn't go away. She should never have agreed to help Tom repair the windmill. Not that he had really given her any choice. He had made it clear that if she couldn't do her share of the work at Mescalero... She shuddered, thinking of the consequences. Then she shuddered again, thinking of her precarious perch on the windmill and the ground far below her.

The way he had described the job, it had seemed so easy. "Not that much to it," he had told her. "The windmill's been the only piece of machinery the cowboy's ever understood."

When she opened her eyes, the ground was still far below, too far—all fifty feet of galvanized windmill.

The horizon stretched out in a shimmering, vibrating haze of heat. Her left hand gripped the rung, but her sweaty palm felt dangerously slippery on the angle iron. Hot wind tugged at her hair and whistled in her ears. It increased her dizziness. Blackness. A growing buzzing in her ears. She felt herself begin to sway.

Tom, shirtless and kneeling on the windmill platform, glowered over the edge at her. "I told you, don't look down. Just pass the pliers up to me."

She fastened her gaze on the pair of cowhide gloves jammed in his back pocket. "I . . . I can't." Her teeth began chattering. At the same time, she couldn't breathe. Her stomach felt like a yo-yo hurtling toward the ground fifty feet below. "I can't . . . move."

He looked over his shoulder at her again. The corners of his sensual mouth curved downward in frustration, but he must have seen the abject terror in her eyes. After a moment he said grudgingly, "All right, hang on. I'm coming over the side."

She squeezed her lids closed. Oh, God. Hurry, Tom!

Overhead she could hear the wind singing against the fan's eight-foot steel blades. The sun was roasting her skin, yet inside she felt as if she would never be warm again. Goose bumps puckered her flesh, and her heart thudded in her ears at a furious speed. A stiffness that could have been rigor mortis was setting in, and her paralyzed fingers began to slip.

Then, all at once, she felt his presence around her, and when she opened her eyes he was facing her. He had managed to swing inside the welded pipe structure.

His warm hand closed over her clammy one. "When I tell you to, I want you to let go."

"I can't!"

"I'll hold you."

"I can't," she wailed.

"Marianna, look at me!" The authority in his voice reached through to her frozen core. "You will!"

"You don't understand," she gasped, tears filling her eyes.

"I understand that you're going to obey me!"

His harsh tone captured her attention. She fastened her gaze on his glittering hazel eyes and hard, flat cheekbones. His eyes controlled her completely. They willed every muscle, every bone, to obey him. Without that total submission to him, she knew she would never make it down safely.

"I want your absolute trust," he said, his voice low, gentle, insistent.

Dazed, she nodded.

"All right, darlin'," he said softly, compellingly. "I'm going to swing around the ladder so that I'm behind you. My body will protect yours."

His hot breath fanned her cheek as she stared sightlessly out at the vast, treeless horizon. He continued to talk in that deep, entrancing voice—as if she were a birthing heifer! "We'll move down the ladder together. You'll be safe in my arms. I'll tell you to move first one foot, then the other. Understand?"

She nodded, but a whimper escaped between her chilled lips. Some peripheral part of her was aware of his muscle-roped arm gathering her in against his solid

length, of his thighs wedging around hers, of his vel-
vet-smooth, sun-heated brown skin.

"Your left foot," he ordered. "That's it. Now your
right one." His tone softened, making his words a
calming southwestern drawl. "That's it, darlin'.
You're doin' real good."

Her panic began to recede. "Twenty-two more
rungs left," he whispered encouragingly. Her body
was tightly imprisoned within the curve of his big,
protective one.

Even as he talked her down, his lips made reassuring forays against her ear. "Seventeen."

He took her lower.

"Now only eight."

All at once she felt the ground come up under one
boot, then the other. He turned her to face him. "It's
all right. You did it. You're safe."

At that instant an enormous weakness sapped
whatever strength remained within her, and she collapsed against him. He caught her limp body in his
arms and carried her over to the windmill's tank.
There he propped her up in the cool shade of its wall.
Perspiration suddenly began breaking out all over her
body, and with his free hand he stroked back the damp
tendrils clinging to her forehead.

Damn it, not again! she thought. First it was all that
blood at the branding, now heights! Her silly weakness had made a fool of her all over again!

She shoved his hand away. "Don't touch me!"

He sat back on his haunches. "Hell, woman, what's
the matter with you?"

She swung at the broad wall of his chest, wild to have a target for her fury at her own incompetence. "You're the one who told me to go up there!"

He gritted his teeth. "You didn't have to come to work on Mescalero."

She scrambled to her feet. "All along you've been goading me—"

Her boot heel slipped on a pebble, and his hand grabbed her wrist. Furious, she tugged at his manacling fingers. "Take your hands off me!"

"Don't be a damned fool. Stop your yelling."

"You knew going up that ladder would terrify me!" She tried wrenching her arm from his grasp.

"I did not." He held her fast, his eyes glinting wickedly. "Ruthie and Rob both work on the windmills. I thought you'd be able to do something as simple as pass me tools."

"Damn you!" The gibe about the ranch women was too much. She struck out. Sweat stung her eyes, blinding her, and her fist only caught his shoulder.

He grunted. "Damn it, will you stop hitting me? Get control of—"

"You get your kicks out of intimidating people?" she shouted. She wanted to throttle him for scaring her half out of her mind up there on that damned windmill. "Out of squashing your convicts beneath your thumb and making them grovel!"

She swung at him again, this time missing completely. He held her away from him while she flailed wildly. "You're as crazy as the rest of those hopped-up Hollywood addicts."

That infuriated her more than anything. Perhaps it was because, like it or not, she valued his opinion and couldn't stand to have him lump her in with the rest of the convicts who had done service duty at Mescalero. She threw herself at him, and they both toppled backward, sending his battered Stetson somersaulting away in the dust. He circled her waist with one steely arm and hauled her off him. Before she could scramble loose, he came up straddling her. He pinned her wrists above her head.

"Let go of me, you muscle-bound oaf!"

"Lord, I hate a nagging woman."

She glared up at him. He was a sexy, chauvinistic cowboy—jeans, no shirt, sweat matting the curly black hair on his massive chest.

"Tell me," he asked dryly, "do you attack all the men you know like this? Your good friend Trent must have scars up one side and down the other."

"Shut up!" she hissed. She tried to buck him off and he sprawled his heavy body atop hers, leaving her stunned. The air whooshed out of her lungs. His powerful length anchored her completely. "You're assaulting me! I'll have you arrested for this!"

"Woman, you're plumb crazy!" His eyes searched her arms, which were stretched above her head and anchored in his handcuff-firm grip. "No needle marks."

"What? Needles? I told you I didn't do drugs!"

He lowered his head to hers. She saw the hard planes of his rough-handsome face, the sexy-mean mouth. By God, he was handsome. Not that she cared. Then he sniffed her breath. At that, the blood pounded in her head. "You go to hell, Tom Malcolm!" she panted. "I'm not drunk! And you're disgusting!"

Her breasts, under the powder-pink T-shirt, rose and fell rapidly. She saw his eyes move down to them and saw the abrupt, knowing slant of his wide mouth. "Get off me," she snapped. She tried to loosen her fists from his grip. "You cruel, nit-witted side of beef!" She hardly knew what she was doing, she was so mad.

He levered himself away from her, and his slashing black brows lowered. "Not a chance. I'm staying here till you cool down, darlin'. And you better believe I can ride the best of the wild mares."

Enraged, she sucked in her breath. Their bodies were pressed together intimately, his thighs clamped over hers to hold her down. Through the red haze of her anger she could feel the heavy pressure of his groin fitting insistently into the vee created by her spread legs. "Don't flatter yourself that you're going to get anywhere with me! I find you totally repulsive!"

She squirmed under him, and the dust flurried around them. He pressed her down until the sand gritted into her buttocks and back and hands. Their sweat and body heat steamed around them.

"You worthless Hollywood airhead," he growled. "As if you could interest me. You've got a pea for a brain, or you never would have gotten involved in drugs to begin with."

She was so blind with fury that she couldn't think straight—and she wanted him so badly that she had lost all reason. She thrashed her legs against his, but he pressed her down easily.

"Don't give me your prima-donna act," he drawled. "Your manufactured sex appeal doesn't turn me on at all. I prefer the real thing."

He had struck through to the core of her emotional turmoil—the fear that she didn't have what it took to be truly and wholly a woman. Only on the surface, before the camera. Hadn't Jax faulted her for being wooden in bed? Tears welled inside her, but her pride staved them off with anger. She grabbed at Tom's hair to force him away. "As if I'd want you!"

He captured her hands, trying to pull them out of his hair. "You're just furious because I'm not after your body like half the casting-couch execs are."

Some mindless creature had control of her. She let go of his hair and writhed beneath him. But her futile attempt to escape only jammed her pelvis upward, toward the hard bulge in his jeans. She was crying with wounded fury.

Something predatory gleamed in his narrowed hazel eyes, darkening them, and tightened the curved, sensual line of his mouth. "That does it! I've taken all I'm going to from you."

"Why, you muscle-bound clod!" Suddenly she was all over him, pummeling, scratching.

"You little redheaded hellcat!"

She drew her nails down his chest and ribs, and she felt his powerful body convulse against hers in surprise, and she clenched her hands tightly on his flesh.

He groaned and pried at her hands. "Let go of me, damn you!"

What was wrong with her? Her body was afire, aching for his. She made herself release him, but in doing so her hand accidentally grazed the zipper of his jeans. With a will of their own, her fingers released the snap, then tugged the zipper downward. His sex sprang free of his briefs, his flesh satiny and hot and throbbing.

She went absolutely still. How had she run amok like that? What in heaven's name was she doing?

Tom stared down at her, veins pulsing at his temples. His breathing was as raspy as hers. His face was strained, a muscle in his jaw twitching. Perspiration broke out across his forehead.

" You've gone and done it," he muttered.

Suddenly she realized she'd gone too far. "I'm sorry," she whispered. "I didn't realize...."

Her words trailed off as she saw his face darken with raw passion. It was as if he had been patiently waiting for this business of play wrestling to be concluded. He lowered his head. "You wanted this."

Then his hard mouth ground down over hers. The desert floor quaked beneath her; the white-hot sky shimmered like a mirage. In a last attempt to salvage her sanity, she pushed against his lips.

"Don't," he muttered against her mouth.

His lips ground against hers. If this was a kiss, it
wasn't like anything in the movies. There was no pre-
tense here. This was sheer lust, savage passion. Its
fierce heat branded her trembling lips.

"Yield," he rasped.

When she tried to turn her head away, his mouth
pressed hard over hers, forcing her head into the sand
and parting her lips wide for him. She moaned, a feeble, muffled objection that she knew she didn't really
mean, but he ignored her. Ruthlessly his tongue
jammed into her mouth and claimed the satiny interior for its own. Its voyage seduced her, mesmerized
her.

Her fists ceased pummeling his back. She was wild
with need. Her fingers crept up past his shoulders and
muscular neck to slide into his thick, rumpled hair. He
felt so good, with his heavy, virile body crushing hers.
She inhaled his smell. Pure man, pure sweat, pure
arousal.

It was obvious who was in control now. His lips still
ravishing hers, he propped his weight on one elbow
and deftly yanked both her jeans and his down to their
ankles, so that their clothing was half on, half off. She
was pinned beneath him, and he didn't even bother to
save her lacy bikini panties. He merely ripped them
down the front and tossed them aside. He had only
one objective in mind.

Her thighs were open to him. His big hands cupped
her buttocks, and he drove inside her soft, secret place.
She was jolted with raw desire that sent the breath
whooshing from her. She whimpered against his ear,

and her fingers dug into his scalp. She could feel him throbbing with passion as he stretched her, invaded her, plunging all the way to ecstasy.

She cried out then, but his mouth clamped down on hers, silencing her. Her inner thighs stretched painfully at their juncture, unused to the demands of passion, yet somewhere inside her a red-hot ember caught fire. Excitement burst within her, swelling her tightly around him.

Guttural sounds rumbled deep in his throat, whipping desire to a frenzy within her, and sweet, hot moisture filled her. The air exploded around them. He nipped her throat. She bit his earlobe. He drove into her with hungry force. She arched back with furious desire.

Ragged words rose chokingly from his throat. Mindless, all she could make were little animal sounds in return. She matched him, need for need, movement for movement. She couldn't get enough of having him inside her.

He couldn't get his fill of her, either. He braced himself on his hands, his arms rigid, his powerful torso heaving above her, and took her with a sweating, grunting ferocity. A savagery took hold of her that threatened to burst her veins. When his great body began shuddering and low animal sounds rushed out of his hot mouth, searing her cheek, her eyelids, she went wild. Flames erupted in her brain and between her thighs. She writhed beneath him. Shamelessly she drew herself tightly around him, refusing to give him up. She matched his relentless fury.

His sweat mingled with hers. "Aw, Marianna. You make it so good."

"Don't you dare stop on me now!"

With that, he went out of control. A savage growl purred from him. His body, crushing hers, bowed up, and he drove into her in one final burst of electrifying energy. Then he fell atop her, quaking with aftershocks. He made small gasping noises against her temple, his breath fanning the sweat-dampened tendrils of her hair.

She sucked air into her starved lungs. Beneath her, the sand abraded her buttocks and shoulders. She realized that her jeans were knotted awkwardly around one ankle. Blindly she gazed up into the white-hot sky, waiting for it to stop spinning.

For one shattering second it had seemed to her that she was on the edge of a precipice, waiting to plummet into the aching void. She had never come close to that explosive completion with Jax.

Tom had almost discovered the painful truth—that her inability to achieve fulfillment made her a sham of a woman, a mere celluloid image. But for one split second she had come perilously close. Tears gathered in her eyes. Why did it have to be with this...this cowboy? Worse, her body still twitched with unfulfilled need.

Tom lifted his head to peer down at her. His hair was curled into wet ringlets plastered to his forehead.

Tenderly he cupped her chin and angled her head so he could see her face. He cleared his throat. "Are you all right?"

She wiped angrily at the betraying tear that had seeped from the corner of her eye. She couldn't look at him, couldn't let him see her weakness for his type of man—implacable, commanding, in charge. And a little dangerous, too. Like a rogue stallion. Or, better yet, that big, satanic-looking bull in the south pasture.

Instead, she turned her gaze on herself, naked from the waist down. Her thighs glistened with sweat and sand.

"Answer me," he ordered, but his deep, rasping voice was curiously gentle.

"Sure, I'm all right," she said bitterly. "It's not every day I wallow in the dirt with the big boss."

The worst thing was that there was no way she could avoid him. She was literally his prisoner. A prisoner of love. She couldn't believe it.

No, a prisoner of sex. That was the only thing that attracted her to him, she insisted. Sheer sex.

His searing eyes narrowed. The frown he wore slowly dissolved. "I think I understand the problem." His fingers deserted their grip on her chin to touch her swollen lower lip gingerly. "You didn't . . . reach satisfaction with me."

Her eyes flashed at him. "Should I have?"

He moved back into a half crouch over her. "There haven't been that many men, have there?" he muttered, as if he weren't really expecting an answer.

"Of course not, you stupid jackass!" Tears were streaming down her face now. She couldn't look at him. Instead she stared at the wiry hair that wreathed one masculine nipple. "I'm a professional actress, not a honky-tonk whore."

He shook his head, as if clearing it. "Don't tell me. Only one—that rock-star husband of yours." Even as he spoke, he began drawing off the jeans that were tangled around her ankle. "Right?"

"What are you doing!"

"What I should have done in the first place." He reached to tug off her T-shirt. His hands unlatched the front bra clasp with practiced ease. "Given you what you needed." He drew in his breath in a sharp gasp. "You're beautiful!"

She sat up abruptly. Her breasts swung free. Aghast, she clamped her hands over them. "No! I mean, I don't need anything."

"Yes, you do, honey," he said in that low, husky, soothing voice. Then he was kneeling over her again. His big naked body, with all those sexy, smooth muscles, was blocking out the burning sunlight. His skin was a healthy sun-brown, his chest a broad expanse of steely flesh. Lighter flesh well below the iron-hard plane of his stomach marked the line of his low-slung jeans. And lower... She closed her eyes and bit back a groan of need at the sight of his arousal.

Her gaze skittered back to that wolfish mouth, lifted at one end in a knowing smile. He gently removed her hands from her breasts and replaced them with his. She trembled at the roughened touch of his palms on her painfully erect nipples.

"If this had to happen," he purred, "then, by God, it's gonna happen right."

The hard, frantic caresses of earlier were forgotten now. He eased her back down onto the ground, stretching out beside her. He propped his head on one hand. The strong, blunt fingers of the other lazily circled her breasts in sensual motions, and her skin puckered at once in response.

" . . . boggles my mind that one of the screen's most sensuous women doesn't know the first thing about sex. You don't, do you?"

"That's not . . . true." But it was useless to waste the words denying it, especially when breathing was almost impossible at that moment.

His fingers followed the slight mound of her stomach, penciled by the faint lines of stretchmarks. "You're more of a lady than I've ever laid eyes on, darlin'. You just haven't been made a woman yet."

"I haven't ever . . ." She closed her eyes. " . . . done this before." Not this way. Not for the pure pleasure, not for the exquisite sensation of just *feeling*!

"I believe it," he rumbled. His hand trailed down over her rib cage. "You've been neglected, haven't you?"

Then his touch moved to her inner thighs, and delicious shudders rippled through her. She was a passive prisoner. "No, I've had—" she sucked in her breath at his touch "—lots of men."

"Liar," he rasped. "It should have happened this way to begin with, but Lord Almighty, I swear I didn't know you wanted this."

"I don't."

"I don't believe you." His fingers eased into her moist cleft.

Sudden fierce heat radiated through her, like the aftershock of an atomic detonation, and she gasped. He leaned over and brushed her parched lips with his. Her legs spread treacherously for him. She wanted his heavy body atop her again, wanted him, just wanted him. She squirmed against the hard shaft jutting along the curve of her hip.

"No, darlin'," he murmured into her mouth. "First things first."

She twisted her head away. "It won't work!" she sobbed. All the frustration of Jax's futile attempts crowded in on her. Long, dry, painful nights of trying, just trying, and—nothing.

"Listen, Marianna, your husband tried to make it too damn complicated." His thick finger stroked the damp tunnel of her flesh, and she went rigid. "Stop fighting it," he coaxed. "Give in to me, darlin'. Trust me the way you did up there on the windmill."

And, as it had on the windmill, his voice wove its magic within her. She accepted the fingers that stroked her. Her eyes closed, she smelled his musky heat. Unknowingly her hand reached out for that hard length of flesh, then drew away as if burned.

"Go ahead, darlin'. Hold me. Love me, too."

At her tentative touch, his mouth quickly possessed hers, his tongue doing what he wouldn't yet let the rest of himself do. Entering, thrusting, arousing her in violent tempo with his fingers—and her hand moving on him.

She couldn't stand the waiting. Her breath, as well as his, was ragged. She strained against him, her hand frantically raking his chest. A whorling vortex of darkness sucked her into a blackness that exploded with vibrant colors. She sobbed out.

"Hang on!" he whispered, and before she could object he withdrew his fingers and plunged his full engorged length deep inside her. It feels so good, she thought, and then she forgot to think at all. Sweat dripped off him onto her. The muscles across his back and shoulders bunched with each mighty thrust. Her legs wrapped around him, anchoring him to her.

She cried out against the hollow of his neck, tasted his salty skin, breathed his musky smell. Desire flamed like wildfire between her legs. That elusive, tumultuous feeling charged through her body, jolting her. Blindly she searched for his mouth. Her lips parted and wildly claimed his. She met his low growl with an animal shriek of her own as he poured himself into her.

She lay dazed, mellow, floating. She couldn't quite believe what had happened. Tom had been tender and considerate, wild and strong. She slid a furtive look at him, his face nuzzled against her collarbone, his wet hair tangling with her own.

"It was good, wasn't it?" he said lazily, triumphantly male.

She couldn't let him know the power he had over her now. The power to make her feel fully and wholly a woman. Whatever it took, however much it hurt, she had to keep him from knowing. "It was great with a little *g*," she replied indifferently.

Chapter 9

On the ranch, the seasons were defined by the tasks that had to be done. Following the spring roundup and branding came the labor of summer: fixing dams, digging postholes, stringing fences, building corrals.

Rob chafed at the restraint her broken wrists put on her activities. She had always taken pride in her superb physical condition, but now, even though the casts had been removed from her wrists, she lacked her former strength. She was reduced to doing the lightest work around the house and yard, and then only with care. Since school was out, Shyloh was free to help around the sprawling place, making the work easier for Rob, but not any more pleasant. She was definitely not a woman bred to domesticity.

Rebelliously she observed from the veranda as Marianna rode out every day with the ranch hands.

Rob was accustomed to riding herd on the men, and it burned her that the men complacently accepted this female intruder despite Marianna's less-than-out-standing performance as a ranch hand.

"She doesn't even know how to dally a rope," Rob muttered one morning as she watched the crew saddle up.

"With face like that," Red Eye said, winking at Shyloh, who was sitting beside him, "a woman don't need to."

Rob shot a disgusted glare at the old Indian. "Whose side are you on, anyway?"

He pushed his creaking old bones up from a pine-slab bench, worn smooth from years of use. "Whichever side has the most firewater."

She thudded her fist against his scrawny shoulder. For her, the gesture was one of affection, and everyone at Mescalero understood that. "You old hooch hound. You've got so much juice in you, your brain's pickled."

So was someone else's, for that matter, she thought grimly. And he was a man who rarely drank. Her narrowed gaze switched to the yard, where her brother was giving instructions to the hands that morning. Marianna was going out on her own, riding fence along part of the thirty or forty miles of the south rim pasture.

Rob's mouth twisted. That particular string of fence, built within the last ten years, required little maintenance. It had solid posts and good galvanized wire. *The woman's totally useless! Helpless! I can just* imagine her trying to repair rusted wire and posts so rotten they won't even hold a staple anymore.

"All right," Tom was telling Marianna. "Load up on staples and take a hammer. All you have to do is tack up the barbed wire where the staples have popped out. And don't go getting any ideas about the direction you're riding. Cross that border and I'll track you down, I promise."

Bobby elbowed a grumpy Emmitt. Rand and Colt slanted covert glances at each other. Fireworks were once again in the making.

"There's not enough money in the world to make me head for Mexico, *Mr.* Malcolm!"

From the early-morning shadows, Rob's critical eye fell on Marianna: soft skinned, her womanly, rounded figure accentuated by the tight jeans and her face still becomingly flushed from a sound sleep, despite the irritation that smoked in her gray eyes at that moment.

Or was it Tom's wolfish gaze that elicited that blooming vitality that had been noticeably absent when Marianna had first arrived three months before? Both of them looked as if they were holding themselves back from a free-for-all, yet straining at the bit at the same time.

Some nights in the desert, when a storm boiled up out of the southwest, the lightning put on a show that no amount of Hollywood special effects could duplicate. Bolts of blue-white seemed to vibrate to the bone. The very air crackled with electricity. And that was how it was now, Rob thought, frowning as she watched her brother and that movie star.

A sick feeling curled inside her stomach as the ranch hands rode away without her. She had never been sick a day in her life—until that McKenna woman had given her the wretched flu!

Rob couldn't imagine life anywhere other than Mescalero, the only place she felt really secure in herself. The need to reestablish herself with the land, to feel Mescalero's sun on her face and wind in her hair, was overpowering. It had been months since she'd checked on her portion of the ranch.

She thrust the apron at Red Eye. "You can play squaw today and do the breakfast cleanup. I'm driving out to Slaughter Mesa."

"Can I go with you?" Shyloh asked.

She was such a skinny child, Rob thought. All legs, and a pinched face with those huge eyes and that bushy hair. "It's a tough ride in the sun, and the Dodge isn't air-conditioned. Besides, you'll miss your afternoon nap. Your mom might not want you out."

"Oh, please. I want to see the rest of Mescalero. Pleeease?"

"You couldn't see it all in three days, hon." Hands on her hips, she stared down at the pale child. Maybe it was because she and the girl were both outcasts of a sort, but Rob made up her mind. She reached out and ruffled the girl's unmanageable yellow hair. "Okay, you can go. But don't come bellyaching to me if your mom gets all riled up. You're on your own, buffalo gal."

"Oh, I can take care of myself, all right," Shyloh said with the elaborate dignity of a child who has been around grown-ups for most of her life. "Do I really look like a buffalo?"

Rob headed off toward the pickup, wryly amused by the kid by her side, who matched two skipping steps to her one long stride in order to keep up. "Buffalo? Well, with all that woolly yellow hair, yeah. But a white buffalo. That's special. The Indians thought a white buffalo was good magic, because it was rare."

Shyloh seemed to think about it. She climbed into the Dodge pickup and nodded her head sagely. "Y'know, Miss Malcolm, I like that—buffalo gal."

"Make that 'Rob,' buffalo gal."

As Rob had warned, the drive was a long one, and not just for Shyloh. Her own wrists hurt just from trying to control the bouncing of the pickup over the back roads, mostly caliche trails laid down by oil crews drilling wells, a few of which had hit pay dirt. But most of them had been dry holes. Come Monday, she decided, she'd make Tom let her go back to work.

Several times she cast sideway glances at the girl, but Shyloh seemed to be taking the rough ride in stride. Her little hands clutched the sun-heated metal door each time the pickup dodged a windblown tumbleweed, skirted a rotted yucca or leaped an unexpected gully.

"Where'd you get the name Shyloh?"

"From a movie my mom made. *Sundown at Shiloh*. It's some battleground, something to do with the

Civil War, she says. Only she spelled it different. Where did you get the name Rob?''

''It's really Roberta. Named for my pa, Robert Edward Malcolm. Just think, I could have been called Edwarda.''

The girl tilted her head, studying Rob's profile. ''Well, Rob seems to fit better than Ed.''

Rob laughed—for the first time since the arrival of the McKenna woman and her daughter. ''I won't argue with you about that.''

Rob's twenty sections were separated from the main portion of Mescalero by the lower part of the White Sands Missile Range. The government had taken over that section, and her Grandma Ella, along with other area ranchers, had filed a lawsuit, which was still pending in the courts after forty years. She only vaguely remembered her grandmother, but the old woman was her role model: strong, courageous, hardworking.

An extra forty-five minutes were lost by taking the main highway that detoured around that part of the missile range. The early Spanish settlers had given Rob's portion of Mescalero the name of Cerro de la Matanza. *Matanza* meant a massacre or wholesale killing, a reference to the fierce Apache warriors who had fought in the area. *Cerro* meant a lone mountain. Somehow Slaughter Mesa as the Anglos had come to call it, had become the subject of a grisly legend and was said to be haunted.

Rob turned off the pickup engine and silently stared at the dilapidated line shack, shed and corrals at the mountain's base. A harsh heat lay over the baked adobe and dull sagebrush.

"Is it really haunted?" Shyloh asked beside her. "For reals?"

At that, Rob chuckled. "Well, I've never seen a ghost there, though I'm sure old Red Eye has, when the DTs get the better of him."

"DTs?"

"The shakes. When Red Eye was young, he used to smuggle contraband liquor across the Mexican border during Prohibition."

"Prohibition?"

Rob revved up the Dodge once more and started toward the line shack. "Yeah—when it was illegal to sell liquor in the United States. A long time ago. Anyway, Red Eye was hiding out in the line shack when he met Grandma Ella. You have to remember, he was a young man then. Fierce and strong and handsome."

"Did they get married?"

"Nope. Grandma Ella was already married and had a son, my father Robert. Once married, always married, was the way Grandma Ella was raised. Not like these Hollywood people who divorce and remarry whenever the whim takes them."

The hurt look in Shyloh's face made Rob regret her barb. "Anyway, after Grandpa died, Grandma Ella ran the ranch single-handedly. And Red Eye came and went when the notion struck him. He wasn't the kind to be tied down. But when Grandma started getting sick, he just upped and moved in with us. Not even a by-your-leave. Been here ever since, 'cept for a spell after she died. Then he headed out for somewhere. I've got a feeling he came here to stay with the ghosts. Her ghost, maybe."

"I like that story," Shyloh said, her pinched, angular face almost soft. "Better than any movie."

"Just a story." Rob didn't mean to deflate the girl's enthusiasm, but there was no use in putting foolish ideas in her head about love and all that. Sooner or later the girl would learn different. Besides, the girl's head had probably been stuffed full of fantasies already by those film people.

"Come on, buffalo gal. Let's take a look-see around my place. Find out how run-down it's gotten since last time I was here."

With Shyloh following, Rob slid between the railings of one corral, the only one left fully standing. A good bodark post would last forty or fifty years, but this gate, supported by only one hinge, teetered crazily in the hot breeze. Such a vast silence hung over the place that the sand could actually be heard rustling against the pockmarked adobe walls of the crumbling line shack.

"Spooky," Shyloh muttered. "It really is haunted, isn't it!"

"Only by wasted yearnings."

"What does that mean?"

Rob pushed open the door, and it creaked eerily. A shadow scurried across the rotten weatherboard floor, and Shyloh squeaked.

"Just a desert packrat," Rob said. She glanced around at the cobwebs draped across a broken window filmed with dirt, at the rickety table that tottered on three legs, at the mattressless iron bedstead and the potbellied stove, which had collapsed in on itself. "Yep," she muttered. "This place sure has taken a turn for the worse."

She crossed the plank floor to the window and ran a finger down the dust-coated pane. Her dream of establishing a quarter-horse ranch where she would both breed and train her horses, as well as other people's— the kind of operation that would eventually produce a world champion cutting horse—looked like the present view from the dirty window: dim. A lot of work and a lot of money would have to be poured into the old place.

"Yuk!" Shyloh said.

Rob turned around and saw the object of the girl's attention near the doorway: a scorpionlike creature a good six inches long equipped with a massive pair of pinchers. She chuckled. "It's called a vinegaroon, 'cause when it's smashed, it gives off a vinegar smell."

Shyloh stared at it with morbid fascination. "Anything so ugly's got to hurt you."

"Naw. It's not poisonous." She shot a thoughtful glance at the girl. Suddenly an idea hit her. "Buffalo gal, get me that tin can over there under the bed. We're taking that vinegaroon back to Bronco Bobby. He likes to collect critters like this."

After Shyloh collected the tin can, Rob cornered the harmless creature between the door and the wall and deftly scooped it into the can, pushing down the partially opened lid to imprison it.

"Gosh, you're really neat, Rob. You're not afraid of anything, are you?"

Shyloh wasn't expecting a response, but Rob could have talked about her own private fears, of not being able to cope with the outside world, of being made a fool, of being left alone with no one to love her.

On the drive back to the ranch house, Shyloh did a lot of talking, mostly asking questions. "What was Colt's mother like?"

"Pretty. Quiet. Sad."

"Why?"

"There was bad blood between her and our father. And besides, she didn't fit into the Malcolm world."

Just as Tom wouldn't fit into that McKenna woman's fast-paced world. One way or another, Rob vowed, I'm gonna save him from making a fool of himself.

Tom stretched his long body out over the space of four bleachers and, hands clasped behind his head, turned his gaze up to the stars. They filled the vast sky. But even if he had a buck for every star he could see, it still wouldn't be enough to keep the ranch running the way it should be. By the time he passed his share of Mescalero into Rand's and Colt's hands, it probably wouldn't be worth keeping.

Not unless ranching was in the boys' souls: the love of solitude, of working with nature, of watching the changes of the seasons and observing wildlife.

Not unless Mescalero was in their blood.

He had never wanted anything as much as he wanted Mescalero. Not riches, nor glory, nor power. Now, though, he wanted something else. He wanted Marianna McKenna. It was all he could do to keep his hands off her, to keep his mouth from crushing her lovely lips and his fingers from twining through that devil-red hair.

He was lusting after her. Even now, the heat of wanting her steamed within him, turning in on itself, immensely powerful, dangerous. He had done the very thing he had warned his ranch hands against. But how the hell was he supposed to have known that beneath that sophisticated exterior, that professional beauty, was such a soft, vulnerable and innocent woman?

He wished he had never witnessed her compassionate act, placing the dead barn owl in the tree. It would have been so much easier to scorn her as a superficial hedonist. And to scorn himself for being drawn to her.

Without really straining, he could hear the muffled slam of the kitchen screen door and knew she had finished the supper dishes. She would avoid coming to the arena, imagining that he was probably there, as he was most evenings. She had avoided him ever since that afternoon of frenzied lovemaking beneath the windmill.

As he had avoided her.

He heard her soft steps crossing the yard toward the cluster of bunkhouses. From the farthest cabin, where Bobby, Emmitt, Rand and Colt were playing poker, came raucous laughter and a radio's muted country-and-western music. Red Eye and Shyloh were still in the big house, playing a game of checkers, and Rob was no doubt in the barn, feeding Apache Belle. There were several places where Marianna might choose to while away her evening, but the arena grandstand certainly wouldn't be one of them.

Her footsteps faded, then disappeared altogether with the shutting of her bunkhouse screen door. He tried to fix his attention on other things: the feeder calf auction in Deming two months away; the bald-face yearling steer that had been blinded in one eye by pinkeye; the rising price of feed.

Yet even here he was thwarted. Marianna's scream tore into his thoughts. At once he was up and running, his spurs ringing with every loping stride that carried him to her bunkhouse. Had Bobby gotten drunk and followed her inside? A vision of the young cowhand kissing Marianna flashed behind Tom's eyes, and a red haze of anger clouded his mind. He felt a tremendous urge to beat the kid senseless.

He almost tore the screen door off its hinges. He found her in the back bedroom, cowering in one corner. For a moment he couldn't take his eyes off her. She still wore her jeans, but she had already removed her blouse and bra. Her breasts swayed free, ripe and firm, and their dusky-rose nipples taunted his feverish imagination.

Wide-eyed with horror, she was unaware of her tantalizing state of undress. She edged around the turned-down bed, clinging closely to the wall and flung herself at him. "That . . . that creature!" she gasped.

He held her by the arms, separating her from himself by inches because he didn't trust himself at that moment. Blood pounded furiously in his temples.

"I hate it here. Hate it!" She began pummeling his chest. Tears welled in her eyes. "Do you understand? This place is loathsome!"

"Hey, hold it! What's going on?"

She pointed a trembling finger toward the bed, and a little whimper escaped her lips.

He would humor her. He set her to one side and crossed to the bed, flinging back the covers. There, in the center of the mattress, was the source of her hysteria. "It's only a whiptail scorpion. A vinegaroon. They're harmless."

She shuddered violently. "What's it doing between my sheets?"

He advanced no her slowly, calmingly. "It must have gotten mixed up in the bedcovers this morning."

"Are you kidding?" she demanded shrilly. "I would have noticed something that big and horrid!"

"Mom?" Shyloh's voice came from the front room, but they could both hear her footsteps coming closer.

Marianna grabbed her blouse from the floor and held it in front of her, then turned to see Shyloh in the doorway. The little girl's expression betrayed her anxiety. Something was wrong with her mother!

"It's all right, Shyloh," Marianna managed to say in a reassuring voice, but Tom could tell that she was barely holding herself together. "I just found a . . . an insect between the sheets, and Mr. Malcolm—" she shot him a venomous glance "—was nice enough to offer to remove the ... the thing for me."

Shyloh took a step closer. Then her mouth crimped. "Oh, that. Rob and I found that today. Yucky, isn't it? It's a—"

"I know what it is," Marianna snapped. "How did it get here?"

Shyloh shrugged bony shoulders. "Beats me, Mom. Rob was going to give it to Bobby. Guess it got out of the tin can she put it in."

Marianna knew she could accuse Rob until she ran out of breath but the accusations would get her nowhere. Now she merely watched the young woman warily from the corner of her eye. If Rob had her way, Marianna would be lying in the path of that hay mower right this moment.

Didn't anyone ever rest at Mescalero? It was the hottest part of July, and everyone was in the irrigated alfalfa patch, working. "Haying season," Emmitt grumbled as he walked by, as if that explained everything.

Marianna paused, pushed back her hat and watched Tom, who was driving the mower. The way the dried alfalfa went down in long windrows was pleasing to her creative eye. Behind the mower, Rand drove the baler, and like some miniature factory, the machine shot out neat blocks of wire-bound hay. But the pleasant pastoral scene didn't detract from the clouds of dust that rolled back to choke her and Rob and Colt. Dressed in hay chaps, they were all lifting the bales and tossing them onto the flatbed trailer, which was pulled by Emmitt's pickup.

It had to be at least 110 degrees out. The day was sultry and steaming-hot, with thunder rumbling in the distance. When lightning fringed the clouded horizon like a broken promise, Tom raised his hand, calling a break from the afternoon mowing.

Marianna looked at the sweaty faces around her—all as black as coal miners', as hers undoubtedly was, too. Sweat ringed their underarms. She was covered with gritty dust and twigs of hay. Her hands, though gloved, hurt terribly, cut by the baling wire. And if it wasn't her hands, then it was her back. Every vertebra screamed with pain.

The baled hay hadn't seemed that heavy at first. But by midday she would have sworn the bales weighed a ton each. Rob had moved easily, her arms hefting the bales with a rhythmic motion that told of many years of practice. Marianna had decided then and there that she would be damned if she would utter one word of complaint.

Tom, Rand and Emmitt joined them at the back of Emmitt's pickup, which was loaded with a five-gallon water can. No one talked. They were too tired. Each took a turn at the spigot, filling the tin cup attached by twine. Marianna thought that water had never tasted so good. She could feel its chill all the way down her esophagus.

Whatever cooling effects the water might have had were instantly negated when Tom took his turn at the spigot. Instead of filling the cup, he took off his shirt and drenched it with water. The sight of those sweat-sheened muscles triggered flashbacks of the afternoon at the windmill. Her eyes fixed on his flat belly, the way the damp hair wedged down past the low band of his jeans. Blind desire poured through her.

When he shrugged back into the wet shirt, it clung to his torso, outlining the pronounced chest muscles and powerful biceps. His broad shoulders strained the shirt's seams. He wiped his hand down his lean stomach, rivuleted with sweat, and she swallowed thickly.

This desperate wanting must be like what a drug user feels, she realized. Once you've tasted, you're hooked. You want it over and over again, until you'll do anything to have it. Until it destroys you.

"Break's over," Tom said. "Let's finish before the rain hits."

Her eyes lifted from his hair-wreathed navel to meet his flat gaze. Since the afternoon when they had made love, they had both avoided meeting each other's eyes. "You're lagging behind the others," he said in an impersonal tone that stung her. "Want Emmitt to spell you for a while?"

Damn him! "No. Now that I've rested, I can catch up."

She glanced away and met Rob's sly stare. I won't cry! I won't! she vowed silently.

Damn all the Malcolms to hell!

Chapter 10

For Tom, one of the more pleasant summer jobs was riding pastures. "Prowling," was what Emmitt called it, an old-time and highly descriptive word for riding around and looking for problems. In the winter prowling wasn't necessary, because the cattle could be looked over every day on the feed ground.

In the heat of summer, though, when most of the cattle were gathered around the windmills and what few water holes there were, the hands would mount up and ride out to study the grass and the range conditions to determine if the pasture was being overgrazed, check the windmills and water holes to see if the cattle had an adequate supply of clean water and make sure salt licks were available.

Years of ranching had taught Tom to observe any unusual patterns in the movement of wildlife. If he saw a buzzard in the sky or a coyote moving around in daylight, it might mean nothing. Or it might mean that scavengers were feeding on a dead animal. If that was the case, he had to find the carcass and determine the cause of death.

He reined in on the rocky outcrop overlooking the Cinnabar pasture and inspected the cattle bunched there, checking brands, udders, ear tags, everything. The pasture was small enough that he quickly got a count and wrote the tally down on a matchbook cover. For every cow he counted, he made the assumption that there was a calf with her, so he was able to count more quickly, and the number he wrote down was twice what he'd actually counted.

The August afternoon was ungodly hot, and he was sweating like a whore on cowboy payday. He removed his straw summer Stetson to wipe his forehead with the back of his arm. After he clamped the hat back on his head, he skimmed a last scrutinizing gaze over the pasture—and frowned at the sight of a thin plume of dust drifting upward. His teeth clamped down hard on his unlighted cigar. "Well, damn," he muttered.

Riding toward him was a woman. Rob had driven into Deming to sell some dry cows. This woman had to be... Yes, there was no getting around the fact that Marianna McKenna was riding like trouble into his life. He drew one leg over the pommel and lounged, waiting for her. Beneath him, the big black horse pranced restlessly. Without shifting, he brought the animal under control with his knees. "I've got the same feeling you do, Ghost Rider."

As Marianna drew nearer, she slowed the canter of her mount. Beneath the brim of her hat, a wary expression narrowed her eyes, tightened her lips. Close up, in the sunlight, he saw, stunned, that flecks of green and gold glinted in what he had thought of as pure gray irises. They were fascinating eyes, with depths a man could never plumb.

He tipped his hat, his politeness a mockery. "Afternoon, Miss McKenna."

Her gaze dropped, almost shyly. The action intrigued him. An actress, shy? His eyes traveled from her flushed face to the open neck of her work shirt and the full thrust of her breasts. In response, he felt the hardening at the top of his thighs.

"I...I wanted to talk with you." Her voice was soft, as soft as her lips. "Privately."

He forced his gaze away from that enchanting, graceful mouth. "Well, now, I'd say we couldn't get much more private than this, with only the cows to hear. What is it you want to say?"

"What I mean is..." She paused, looking away. "Can we get down and talk a while?"

He stared at her intently. "All right." He dismounted and watched as she did the same. He could have helped, but he knew that if he touched her just once, he'd end up taking her then and there.

She turned to face him, bit her lip nervously and toyed with the reins between her gloved fingers.

"Well?" he asked.

"Can we sit?"

He grunted, hunkered down in a patch of blue gama grass and waited. She took her time, tugging off her gloves. She still didn't seem able to bring herself to look at him. Finally she curled her legs up under her and leaned back on one palm. Her breasts rose and fell rapidly. He remembered too well these pouting white breasts. She shifted under his scrutiny. He was good at waiting. Patience was one of his few virtues. But apparently not where Marianna McKenna was concerned.

The horses, bored, ambled away to graze on the tufts of grass that pushed up through the rocky ground. She seemed to be watching them, but after several long, taut minutes, she whispered, "It's not working out."

"What's not?"

She removed her hat and nervously fanned herself. But from beneath those tangled black lashes, her gray-eyed gaze strayed to the faded skintight jeans that strained over his thighs and his obvious arousal. "Me working here," she mumbled. "I don't fit in."

"This isn't a country club," he growled. Her hair caught fire in the sunlight, and he almost reached out to tangle his fingers in those wild curls. "If I remember rightly, we played this same scene a couple of months back or more, only in reverse. You were begging me to let you stay, then."

She was the one who reached out, impulsively touching his chest. "Please, can't you see this is all wrong?"

He captured her hand and held it imprisoned against his clamoring body. "What do you suggest?"

Her lips trembled. "Let me go. You'd never have to report me gone. Come October, just turn my case file over to the district—"

"No chance, darlin'."

Fury sprang to life in her eyes. She tried to jerk loose. "Let me go!"

"Tell me," he said, pulling her closer until her shoulder was pressed against his chest, "what makes you think I can't have you? Here and now? Whenever I want?"

She stared at him haughtily. "I'd report you for rape, that's why!"

"Even if it were true—which we both know it wouldn't be—who'd believe you? An actress convicted of smuggling drugs into the country? Come on."

He watched her gauge his expression, measuring the relentlessness in it, and saw hope fade from her face. "You always come back to my drug conviction. Have you ever once given me the benefit of the doubt?" she finally asked.

"Why should I?"

For a second, her shoulders slumped. Then her pride rescued her. She began to move away, but he cupped his hand around her neck, staying her.

"I want you," he said huskily. "And it goes against all logic and reason. And you want me, too. Don't deny it. You want me as much as I want you!"

A telltale flush swept her cheeks. "Let go of me! We're not going to start this again."

"We never finished it."

"Damn it, go seduce Ruthie, or someone else who's good at fixing windmills!"

He stared at her somberly, hearing the underlying wistfulness in her tone. He admitted in a grudging voice, "You're working out here better than I expected. You haven't shirked any duty I've placed on you."

His unexpected compliment reached through her anger. She stilled, then rubbed at her temple. "I must be crazy. To let you get to me like this."

"Marianna..."

She trembled, once again starting to draw away.

Something about her set him on fire. He pulled her face down to his. He had meant the kiss to be a retribution—for her contempt of him, for all the nights the image of her haughty face had kept him awake, tantalizing him.

But something went wrong. Instead of claiming her in a fierce, brutal kiss, his lips only brushed hers, tasting, testing, searching...and wanting so badly to feel the same response. He kissed her with a gentleness, a softness, that only a woman like her could bring to the hardened life of a cowboy.

She gave a small moan, and her lips trembled beneath his. He couldn't even be quite sure his imagination hadn't willed it! No! Her mouth grazed back and forth over his. Lightly, oh, so softly, and yielding. Her invitation was answered by his tongue gently edging her lips apart to taste her silky softness.

"Sweet," he murmured against her mouth. "Sweet and soft and giving."

With a shaky breath, she stared up at him. Those hot silvery eyes smoldered with the same sweet, heavy desire. "Please...don't make me beg."

"If I were smart, I'd mount up and ride away from you, woman. Nothing good can come of this."

Her pride stung, she jerked loose and sprang to her feet. He was right behind her, gripping her upper arm and whirling her around to face him. "But I won't. I need to feel you beneath me. Every time you look at me I remember the last time we made love."

"Is that what you call it?" She turned her face up to his. Her lips taunted; her eyes flashed. "I thought that was merely sex."

He moved closer to her. She smelled of some expensive perfume. "Oh, no. It was much more than that. It was the sharing of good feelings, you touching me, me stroking you—" his throat tightened with the overwhelming need of her "—your lovely body."

She shook her head, but it wasn't in denial of his words; it was as if she were trying to shake free of her own desire for him. He could smell that wanting; it intensified the seductive scent of her perfume. "Dear God, I must be out of my mind!" She peered up at him from beneath heavy lids. "Tom," she breathed, "love me."

It was a royal command, not a plea. Still, he cupped her buttocks and pressed her against him, so that she had to acknowledge his arousal. "Is this what you want?" he growled, moving knowingly against her. He needed to hear her admit that she wanted him.

Eyes closed, she nodded.

"Say it, Marianna. Say, 'Tom, please make love to me.'"

She bit her bottom lip. "I told you I wanted you."

His hand found her breast, and his fingers played over the hard button of her nipple. "You told me," he whispered, "not asked me."

"I'm...asking...you." The words were punctuated by little gasps. "Oh, please. Yes."

She was so small, so diminutive, that she brought out protective instincts he'd never known he had. "I know you need this as badly as I do, that you haven't ever been happy in bed with a man before."

She stood rigid, barely breathing, as his lips strung kisses across her jaw and cheek, then up along her temple.

"Believe me, I didn't want this to happen, either. It's against all the rules I've laid down—" his mouth hovered over hers "—regarding prisoners and women, but I can't seem to help myself."

At the touch of his lips, she whimpered. He rubbed his mouth over hers in a nuzzling kiss, dandelion-light, and her mouth opened again for his tongue. She tasted dark and mysterious. He could control the wildest of horses, but he couldn't control himself, the consuming need in him for this woman with whom he had nothing in common.

Desire exploded in him, and he dragged her against him abruptly, deepening his kiss. His hands wound through her hair, tugging her head at an angle to meet his suddenly savage kiss.

Her hands tangled in his hair. "So good," she murmured against his mouth. "I feel so good."

"It's only beginning."

He drew her against him again, but at the feel of his thigh wedged between her legs, parting them, she stiffened, as if partially regaining her senses. Her fingers dug into his shoulder muscles. "You don't even like me...."

"I know, darlin', and you find me insensitive." His hands slid down her slender back to press the flare of her hips into him. "You feel so good, woman."

"Marianna," she said breathlessly into his mouth. "My name is—"

His blazing kiss silenced her. She shuddered as his tongue plunged rhythmically into her mouth, conquering her. She clung to him, her hips arching against him, seeking his hardness. She set him on fire. "Tell me you want me inside you, darlin'."

She shook her head in denial, her fiery hair swishing against his hands on her back. But her words begged him. "Help me!"

His fingers trembling, he began unbuttoning her denim shirt. "Tell me that you want me riding you again and again." He slid her shirt down over her shoulders, creamy-white and soft as a newborn lamb.

"No. Only this last time." But she unconsciously helped him free her arms from the sleeves. "Swear to me."

"I'd swear anything to keep you in my arms," he told her between hot, sweet kisses. His suspicions were confirmed: she wore no bra. Her thrusting breasts beckoned, and his mouth strewed urgent kisses over her satiny skin to one taut pink nipple. His big hand cupped the fleshy underside of her breast, lifting it so that his tongue could gently stroke and draw on the pebbled nipple. She sagged against him, but he caught her and helped her to stand.

"I'll regret this tomorrow," she rasped. Her hands clutched at his hips as his teeth gently scraped the tightened bud of her other nipple.

"Oh, no, darlin'," he said. "Regret anything, but don't regret this." He unsnapped her jeans, their zipper gliding downward. "Let me make love to you, Marianna."

Slowly his hands slid down her jeans. "My panties," she rasped out. "Don't tear them. I don't have that many."

"Don't wear them," he countered in a voice that sounded husky to his ears.

Her panties journeyed down those alabaster legs, long untouched by either sun or man—until that day by the windmill. He sat back on his heels. He couldn't resist her. His face nuzzled the eiderdown-soft curls to inhale deeply of her scent, and then he exhaled great, shuddering breaths. Her fingers dug half-moons into his shoulders, and then, with a little moan that throbbed with desire, her legs buckled.

He lowered her beside him and knelt over her. For a moment his burning gaze measured this incredibly lovely woman, this priceless objet d'art so out of place in his rough, crude world. But her flaming, tousled hair, her kiss-swollen mouth, beckoned him, and with great care his hands slid past her knees to her inner thighs, where his fingers met to cleave the clustered curls and touch the satiny-wet folds.

At his touch, her body suddenly writhed, and she gasped out. Her response triggered hot spasms in him, and fire raced through his veins. "Marianna, unbutton my shirt."

He watched her with a waiting expression. Her fingers trembled as she began, then stopped. Gently he disengaged her hands and finished for her, practically tearing off the shirt before tugging off his boots and jeans. She gazed up at him, her gray eyes smoldering. "When you look at me like that," he muttered, crouching over her again, "I have no regrets at all about the right or wrong of making love to you."

"And will you say that once this is over?" she whispered.

Above them, the sun blazed down, its heat rivaling their own. He stared down into her half-closed eyes, their silvery gleam shaded by her thick lashes. "I'll say that I must be out of my mind," he answered honestly. His hand drew her knee up against his thigh, slick with sweat. "As crazy wild as if I'd spent the afternoon puffing on loco weed."

Her lids lowered.

"Don't," he growled. "Don't think of what it would be like as part of some kind of drug fantasy. This is real. There's no hyped-up excitement here."

Her eyes shot sparks. "I wasn't . . . I never . . ."

He silenced her with his mouth. She murmured something incoherent and tried to push him away, but his tongue found hers, and a jolt of fire seared them both. A breathy sound escaped her lips, and with the soft warmth of her expelled breath, an electric current leaped from her mouth to his. There was no restraint left in him now. He shifted his heavy body over hers, arms braced so as not to crush her. Then he eased inside her, big and hard, his body racked by the need to pour himself into her.

It was a need that wouldn't be held back. Over and over he drove into her, until she was caught up in his mating rhythm. He couldn't help himself, couldn't help the words that tumbled from his feverish lips. "Tell me you want me, want this."

Her legs wrapped around his back, and her neck, slender, porcelain, arched back with the throes of approaching gratification. "Oh, yes!"

"Yes, *Tom*," he prompted, sucking in the dry air like a man about to die."

"Yes, Tom," she gasped. Her arms circled his rib cage, and she cried out wordlessly at his violent possession of her.

Then a scalding oblivion overtook him, and he spilled his seed into her. This time she went over the edge with him, and he held her delicate body against his powerful one as she trembled, went rigid, then finally slack.

He heard her breath, ragged and racing. He rolled off her. It took him several minutes before he could open his eyes. The sky was hazy, and the grass whispered in his ears. He felt stunned. "Darlin'? Are you—"

"Marianna," she corrected. She didn't open her eyes, but her breathing had slowed.

He turned on his side and wrapped an arm around her ridiculously small waist to pull her to him. One of his long legs wrapped around hers as he cradled her against his side. She watched him from between those damnably thick lashes, waiting. He squeezed her tightly. "Now you regret it."

"I'm disgusted with myself for letting this happen."

So, she was the cool sophisticate again. He lowered his head and softly nuzzled the hollow of her shoulder, tasting her, tasting her salty sweat and, yes, even the rich, sensual scent that was exciting him all over again. "Don't be. That's the way the good Lord made us—craving sex." Like her, he wouldn't let himself admit that there was anything more than that in what had happened.

He heard her low chuckle. "All the time? Like right now, even? Again?"

"So you can feel me, hmmm?"

She rolled out of his embrace and sat up. Her fantastic hair, sequined with bits of brush, cascaded around her shoulders. The faint pinkish marks where his teeth had scraped left an interrupted trail on her throat. Gently he touched the marks of his rough caresses.

"No you don't, Tom Malcolm," she said, her eyes widening at the evidence of his renewed arousal. "You're violating the rules you laid down for me!" Anger, directed more at herself than him, turned her eyes to shards of hot ice. "This can't happen again. Do you understand?"

"Right," he grunted. No word had ever cost him more effort.

Chapter 11

The mare had a soft mouth and an even disposition. As a colt, Gypsy had undergone Rob's gentle and patient breaking. Still, Colt Kahze didn't know if Gypsy was ready for Shyloh's inexperienced hand.

"Please, Colt? Can I? All by myself? Rob said it was okay. If you watched me."

Problem was, Rob assumed all females, young or old, were as capable as she was when it came to ranch life. Well, all but Marianna. He felt sorry for the woman. In a way she was as out of her element as he was. And he liked her. Despite the flak she got from Rob and Tom and the others, she wasn't pouting, but was giving the six months her best shot.

Colt nodded his assent and cupped his hands to give Shyloh a foot up.

She shook her head, and the long, straw-colored hair bounced on her shoulders like hundreds of little springs. Her hair was the only thing about her with curves. Her lashes were so thick they hadn't the slightest curl, and her bony body was poker-straight. The little girl fascinated him. She was unlike anything he had encountered on the reservation or among the ranch folks.

"Can I do it myself, Colt?"

With a shrug, he stepped back and caught the reins, just in case. "Go for it, kid."

She wasn't tall or strong enough to pull herself into the saddle easily, but with a little squirming she managed to mount up. He adjusted the stirrups for her spindly legs. Satisfied, he passed her the reins. "Take it easy. Sit deep in the saddle. Let Gypsy go as she chooses 'til she gets the feel of you."

Shyloh shifted in the saddle, set her mouth in a determined line, then nodded. "Gotcha."

He perched on the two-by-six board running along the top fence of the central alley and watched as Gypsy walked slowly and easily around the pen. Then the mare picked up into a jog trot, kicking up little puffs of dust. Shyloh grabbed hold of the pommel, lost the rhythm of Gypsy's stride and began to bounce like a sack of pinto beans.

He called out to her, "Try to think of two rivers. Both running together, each one a part of the other."

Shyloh's elfin face crinkled into an expression of deep concentration, and she loosened her hold on the pommel. At that moment the mare, snorting and tossing her head as if disgusted with its rider, chose to stop short. Shyloh pitched over Gypsy's head. Her body hit the soft earth and crumpled like some rag doll thrown by a child in a temper tantrum.

His heart in his throat, Colt sprinted over to her. He'd seen many a cowboy tossed in the rodeo arena and had himself been piled up by mean-tempered broncs. But Shyloh hadn't been expecting to be thrown and had no experience with rolling landings. He crouched over her and felt her neck for a pulse. Beneath his fingers, it beat steady and strong. She was only stunned. "Shyloh?"

She groaned, and her heavy lashes flickered open. Her big brown eyes looked dazed. "I think I'll stick to the mechanical calf," she mumbled.

"Try to sit up."

"Ohhh." She rubbed her hip. "It feels like my tail-bone's busted."

He grinned. "I doubt it. You're young, and your bones aren't brittle enough."

She glared up at him. "Young? You aren't much older than me, Colt Kahze."

"Five years." He felt centuries older. "Here, get up. That's it." He steadied her with a hand beneath her elbow. "We're going walking. If you don't, you're gonna be as stiff as a newly rosined rope tomorrow."

She took a tentative step. Her face, dirt-streaked, screwed up in pain. "Can't I do this another time?"

"Nope."

She groaned again when she had to bend over to climb between the railings. "My shoulder. It hurts."

"Here, let me see." Gently he ran a practiced hand across her prominent shoulder blades. The bones were small enough to snap like toothpicks. "Nothing out of kilter." He massaged her rigid muscles. "There, that better?"

The expression in her face eased a little. "Yeah."

He steered her toward a trail that rambled through the overgrowth to the old gristmill, its lower level almost hidden by brambles. D.O.G. padded along behind them, his tongue hanging out in the heat. Colt noticed that Shyloh was wincing with each step, and he shortened his stride. They passed a big thicket of wild plums, covered with white blossoms. Come September, there would be plenty of plum jelly.

But Shyloh's mother wouldn't be here to make it. And Shyloh wouldn't be here, either.

"I used to think cowboys were the far-out best," Shyloh grumbled at his side. "Now I think they're just plain stupid." She rubbed her backside gingerly. "Anyone who rides a horse when he could be driving a car has got to be out of his mind."

Colt grinned. "Guess I'm one of the crazy ones. I'd rather have a horse, 'cause it can love you back—no matter what you are."

She halted and put her hand on his sleeve. Her mouth crimped in childish contrition. "I didn't mean that. Not you, Colt. You're special."

Words. He tested her. "Why?"

She jammed her hands in her back pockets and swerved away. "Well," she said, starting to walk again, "'cause you're good with animals...and people, too. You took the pain right out of my shoulder.''

They'd reached the gristmill, whose stone walls were crumbling in spots. "What would you say if I told you I train with a medicine man, a shaman?''

Her eyes widened. "For reals?''

He pushed open the heavy door, and its rusted hinges protested. The musty smell of long disuse whispered over them in a cooling draft. "Yes, for reals. During the school year, after class lets out, I spend a couple of hours every afternoon learning healing ceremonies.''

"Does Tom know?''

She followed him past the giant stone rollers and the empty cornmeal bins. "Is there anything he doesn't know?'' Colt asked. "It was his idea.''

He had expected her to show some interest in the old mill, but instead her attention was fixed wholly on him. "Are you going to be a doctor?''

"Just where would I get the money for medical school?'' he asked, then instantly regretted his sharpness. "Besides,'' he said with an indifferent shrug, "reservation school doesn't exactly prepare its students for heavy-duty studies.''

"You'll be smart enough, Colt.'' She squeezed his hand. "I just know you will.''

He felt uncomfortable. He pulled his hand out of her clasp and pretended not to notice her fleeting expression of hurt. "Come on, let's get you walking again, 'fore you go all stiff on me.''

* * *

That smile of his . . . those work-hardened hands . . . the dark hair that arrowed down the muscular planes of his flat belly.

Marianna couldn't get these images of Tom Malcolm out of her mind. It was even worse sitting scrunched between him and Emmitt in the pickup. Tom's body heat seeped into hers, firing her blood. It was all Tom's fault. He had done this to her.

"You got the list?" Tom asked.

She nodded. In addition to the groceries that couldn't be bought at the trading post, she had listed, at Tom's instructions, such items as laying mash for the hens, windmill leathers, thirty-weight oil and other items needed on the ranch. "Everything that you want is here."

The familiar, faintly mocking look glinted from under the frayed brim of his disreputable black Stetson before he returned his gaze to the road. "Everything?"

The flush that betrayed her as a redhead swept up over her cheeks. She slid a sideways glance at Emmitt, who appeared to be busy stuffing a plug of tobacco into the pouch of his lip. But she suspected he was aware of the sexual current coursing between her and Tom. No doubt the rest of Mescalero was aware of it, too.

A sign proclaimed that Deming, the nearest town to Mescalero, was just ahead. Excitement began to build in Marianna. A real town. With a population of all of thirteen thousand. Maybe. Her lips curved at the irony. A year ago she had been a cosmopolitan woman, bored by the glitter of cities like Milan and Paris, and the mystical allure of the Taj Mahal.

Tom wheeled the pickup onto Gold Avenue and parked first before a saddle and boot shop. Next door was a small department store, with mannequins displaying what passed for the latest fashions in this part of the country. Marianna's eyes weren't drawn to the dated dresses, but to the window artfully featuring cosmetics and beauty supplies. She had run out of her own shampoo and longed to replace the everyday brand used at Mescalero with one made expressly for sun and wind-dried hair. In addition, she needed a moisturizer and nail polish to protect her splitting nails, and many other things that had become luxuries over the past months. What she wouldn't have given for French milled soap.

Tom ushered her into the saddle and boot shop, with Emmitt trailing behind. Quite a few cowhands were browsing along the aisles filled with tack and boots and chaps. Emmitt paused to look at the saddles. His lashes did a jitterbug when he read the price of one.

"Geez," he grumbled. "If a cowboy had some money, he'd go crazy in this place!"

She followed Tom to the rear of the shop, where a multitude of ropes adorned the wall. Above each selection was an identifying plaque: soft-lay nylons, braided nylons, grass ropes, and poly ropes. Tom fingered them, his hands measuring the slightly different feel of each. She knew he would have liked to purchase several but, with Mescalero's financial straits to keep in mind, would eventually settle on only one.

She gathered her courage and asked, "Would you mind if I went next door to the department store?" Her own finances were temporarily in the same condition—due both to the exorbitant cost of the trial lawyers and, before that, to Jax's penchant for living beyond their means. But she could at least enjoy the pleasures of window-shopping.

"Can I trust you?" The words implied that she might attempt to make a run for it, but his lopsided grin totally disarmed her indignation. The way his eyes fastened on her mouth told her how badly he wanted to kiss her.

She flushed under his unswerving gaze. "That should be my line," she said, responding with a grudging smile. Why did she feel as if she were consorting with the enemy?

He looped the rope he'd been testing around her waist. "I think you know that the answer to that is no," he growled. "You *can't* trust me."

"I know," she murmured.

His black brows came together in a frown that she knew was aimed more at himself than her. He released the rope, freeing her. "Meet us out front in ten minutes."

Inside the department store, she wandered along the cosmetic aisles. Her fingers longingly passed over sample bottles of perfumes on a glass tray, toyed with a makeup tester and ticked off the expensive contents labeled on a crystal container of bath oil.

"You wouldn't by any chance be thinking of shop-lifting, would you?"

She whirled at the sound of a man's reedy voice. It belonged to the county sheriff, Cal Reese. Those ball-bearing eyes rolled over her.

She felt again the old humiliation she had come to know in prison, the kind of humiliation that sucked out all of one's pride, leaving the body empty. She hated herself for the fear that she knew showed in her eyes and trembled on her lips. "I was merely look-ing," she managed to get out.

He grinned, but it wasn't the sun-warm grin that etched Tom's mouth. "I could arrest you merely on suspicion of shoplifting. Know that?"

She shook her head wordlessly, feeling her heart fluttering furiously against her rib cage like the wings of a frightened bird.

"That'd be hard to do," Tom drawled, magically appearing at her side. His eyes held the deadly glint of twin pistol muzzles. "'Cause I sent the lady in here especially to make some purchases for Mescalero."

Reese held up the crystal container she had been perusing and appeared to examine it. "Well, now, this here bath oil's awfully frivolous for the likes of you Mescalero folks," he said with a sneer. "And awful damn expensive. Not something on which Mescalero can afford to be squandering what little hard cash it has. Not for a low-quality convict, anyway."

She saw a muscle twitch in Tom's jaw. His hand tightened on her elbow, and she knew he was using all his restraint to keep from shoving his fist into the sheriff's derisive mouth. The slow grin that lifted one corner of his mouth cooled the heat in his eyes. "Reese, you wouldn't know quality if you saw it."

A salesclerk, drawn by the commotion, came over to the counter. "May I help you?"

Tom surprised Marianna by taking out his wallet and calmly counting out four ten-dollar bills onto the counter. "The lady would like the bath oil."

Watching the salesclerk ring up the sale and lay the money in the cash drawer, Marianna felt a sick knot in the pit of her stomach. That was the money Tom had been planning on using for laying mash for the hens and the windmill leathers and that case of thirty-weight oil.

Package in hand, he steered her outside to the truck. His face was a thundercloud. "Get in."

"Tom, I'm sorry."

"Forget it."

He jerked open the door, and she slid in beside Emmitt. The trip to the supermarket was unbearably quiet. She broke the tension of the silence, blurting out, "Look, Tom, I have an idea. I can pay you back—a thousand times over!"

He squinted at her, the kind of look a man gives a slightly unsavory blonde in a too-tight dress. "How? Peddle smack on the streets of Deming?"

"Just listen, damn it!"

Emmitt sat between them, saying nothing and staring straight ahead, blinking rapidly at the cross fire of words.

"With the connections I still have in the film industry," she said, leaning forward to see Tom better, "I can arrange for Mescalero to be used as a shooting location."

Tom wheeled into the supermarket parking lot. "Sure," he growled, getting out of the pickup. "Next thing you know, one of those film people leaves a gate open, the cattle stampede and I have a law—"

She jumped out on her side and came around the back of the pickup to confront him. "As big as Mescalero is, the cast and crew wouldn't be getting in your way. Oh, Tom, at least think about it."

"No way," he said. The way his teeth clamped down on the cigar told her that he wasn't about to relinquish any control, no matter how excellent her idea.

She jerked one of the carts from the rack outside the supermarket. "You're just a stubborn son of a—"

Tom suddenly turned, took two long strides in the opposite direction and caught hold of the collar of a man who was just getting out of a yellow Cadillac. The man, thin and olive-skinned, looked surprised, as did everyone in the vicinity, including Marianna.

"You've been following us since we drove out of Mescalero's gates," Tom charged in a voice that didn't lack the threat of violence, despite its coolness. He eyed the man with the steely glint of a *pistolero*. "I want to know why."

The man, decked out with gold necklace, rings and a bracelet, stuttered, "Why, nothing. I just—I'm a reporter. For the *El Paso Herald*. Wheeler. John

Wheeler. I just wanted to, uh, interview Miss Mc-
Kenna.''

Her eyes narrowed on the man. He looked familiar. Someone so loaded down with gold jewelry wasn't
likely to be forgotten. ''You were at my trial, weren't
you?''

''Yeah. I was covering it.''

She remembered distinctly now. The man had sat
somewhere near the front every day that court had
been in session.

He looked meaningfully at Tom's iron grip. ''Do
you mind? This here's a Dior you're wrinkling.''

Tom frowned, glanced at Marianna. She nodded,
and he loosened his grip on the man's shirt. ''You
want to give an interview to this guy?'' he asked her.

''Hey, look,'' Wheeler said with an oily smile. ''I
could set all the facts straight for you, you know? Tell
your side of the story.''

''I don't know.'' She shook her head slowly. It
would be an opportunity to present the full truth,
maybe to convince someone, anyone, of her innocence. Yet she had learned never to trust the media.
And this man didn't exactly earn her confidence. ''Let
me think about it. Do you have a business card, in case
I want to reach you?''

He dug out his billfold, flipped through the plastic
sheets and said, ''Naw, I'm fresh out. Why don't I just
give you a call in a day or so?''

''I'll give it some thought,'' she hedged. She could
almost feel his eyes boring through her back as Tom
propelled her away.

* * *

The dinner had been a masterpiece of culinary art: leafy spinach greens and sunny circles of carrots had set off the roast with its rich brown gravy and the soft, snowy mound of mashed potatoes. Now that Shyloh had learned to ride and was helping out some, Marianna was spending more time around the ranch house again—and Tom was glad of it.

Glad because she was out of his way. Glad because temptation was being kept at a distance.

Pleasantly full, he stuck a cigar in his mouth and strolled out to the arena. The days were longer now. The soft purple of shadowy twilight colored the distant mountains, and a breeze cooled the after-heat of the day. And it had indeed been one hell of a day, and not just weather-wise.

Usually he enjoyed the occasional trip into town, but he was always ready to leave and get back to the sandhills and sagebrush and the slow rhythms of the animals. But today had been something else.

He propped his elbows on the bleacher behind him and closed his eyes, but he couldn't close out the boiling anger that still bubbled inside him, left over from the encounter with the sheriff. Reese bothered him. The man was a malcontent, had been even as a boy. Tom had heard that in Vietnam, Reese, as a sergeant, had made life miserable for already miserable soldiers. As Luna County's sheriff, he was continuing in that pattern of abusing his position to intimidate others.

Tom crunched down on the end of his cigar. What had really bothered the hell out of him, though, was the galling knowledge that the bath oil was an extravagance he couldn't really afford. Then he remembered the longing, almost childlike look in Marianna's eyes. He wanted to indulge that longing, but he knew with a bitter certainty that he would never be able to satisfy it, not in a thousand years. The blunt truth was that he'd never be able to afford to give Marianna the kind of life to which she was accustomed.

Maybe that was why he wanted to drive Reese's chin all the way up into his Neanderthal brain. But he couldn't allow himself that pleasure, because Reese might just decide to make things more difficult for Marianna than they already were.

Then there was that reporter, that Wheeler dude....

What Tom had been listening for all along—the soft slamming of the screen door—interrupted his speculation on the reporter. Soon Tom heard Marianna's footsteps moving along the path, taking her as close as she would get to him before she veered off toward the bunkhouses. He would have sworn that a faint hint of her perfume wafted with the evening breeze toward the arena. Moments later he heard the muted clicking of her cabin door. The evening seemed suddenly empty without her scent, without her footsteps.

He thought of Rob, who after dinner had taken Shyloh to the trading post to teach her how to play pool. He could no more help himself than he could help breathing. He got to his feet, stretched, tossed away the cigar and started toward Marianna's quarters.

Chapter 12

She stared at Tom through the screen door. Her gaze skittered to the mat of hair exposed by the open shirt, veeing as far downward as the bottom two buttons above the low-slung jeans. They fitted his narrow hips like a second skin, leaving little to her wayward imagination. In the darkness of the porch, his eyes glittered. "I need you."

Her hand went to the folds of her white terry-cloth robe, just below her throat, where her pulse beat erratically. "No," she whispered. "You don't need anyone, Tom Malcolm."

He opened the screen door and stepped inside the darkened room.

She should have latched it in the first place, but she imagined Freud would have said she had been wanting this all along. Regardless, she fought her libido.

She backed up a step, saying, "I was just getting ready to take a bath."

He didn't take his eyes off the low décolletage of her robe. "Yeah, I can smell the bath oil."

"Bath oil?" she murmured vaguely, her gaze fixed on the heat in his hungry eyes.

"What I forked out thirty-seven bucks for today."

"Look, I'll pay you back. As soon as I finish the service duty program. As soon as I get back to acting." She knew she was babbling, but she couldn't help herself. He was so damn sexy. Where was her self-control when she needed it?

"The money doesn't bother me. You do."

They stared at each other. He was giving her time to refuse him. Maybe he was hoping that she would. She tried. "We've been through this before," she said, striving for dignity. She reached up, as if to flick on the light switch. "And all the talking only ends in—"

"Leave the light off." He inclined his head toward hers so that their cheekbones almost brushed. She heard him inhale deeply. "You smell of sweet grass and soap. So clean."

She had sworn never again to let him touch her, had vowed not to let him goad her into losing her temper so that she lost all control of herself as well. But this gentle, almost poetic side of him might well be her undoing. "Go away." She turned her face from his. "Leave me alone."

He backed her into the wall. The muscles of his long thighs pressed against her hipbones. His great body overpowered her. "Is that what you really want?" he said in a low, quiet voice, and nuzzled her neck.

He was a sorcerer. His wizardry left her weak one moment, then turned the knot in the pit of her stomach to a sweet, liquid fire the next. She tried to block out the insidious feelings that left her hopelessly enslaved by his sensual domination. He towered over her. The warmth of his big body reached her through the terry cloth. She couldn't make out his face, but she could recall the sun-streaked hair that was shot with silver, the hazel eyes and the way they made love to her body. She could visualize him naked—how magnificent his body was, its raw masculinity and virile lines. Much more of this and she wouldn't be able to resist touching him.

"The bathwater. It's running."

He sifted her hair through his fingers in a lingering caress, as if delighting in its texture. "All I could think of this evening was how much pleasure you would take in the bath oil, how your skin would glisten like a honey glaze, how soft it would feel beneath my fingers. Damn it, Marianna, I can't keep my mind on what I'm doing these days, because of you. The ranch hands think I've gone raving mad, that I'm an absolute lunatic."

The tone of rough yearning in his voice caught her by surprise. Why did she feel this tenderheartedness for him? She would be leaving in a little over a month. He knew it. But he also knew what he did to her. Knew how he could make her crave his loving with a simple word, a mere touch. So why did he bother to say these things to her? She didn't want him to become dear to her, didn't want to worry about how mercilessly he drove himself to make ends meet.

She struggled against her feelings and nudged him away, but with no result. "You're squashing me!"

He stepped back. "I don't want to hurt you." His voice was unexpectedly gentle. Still, he didn't take his hand from the back of her neck, where his fingers rubbed concentric circles, tingling her nape. His tracker's eyes glowed in the dark. "I don't understand what it is about you. You're useless, spoiled, as fragile as a downy Mexican thistle. But I want you again."

She shook her head, trying to shake off his intoxicating words. "No. No more."

His hand slid from her neck downward, traveling along the valley between her breasts.

"What about Ruthie?" she demanded, seeking anything that might distract him, though her breasts ached for his touch.

His hands shaking, he unknotted her belt and pushed aside the front panels of her robe. "Just friends," he muttered against her arched throat.

"I bet."

"Hell, darlin', don't you think I'd have married Ruthie by now if there was anything more?" Quickly he cupped one breast possessively, gently squeezing its fleshy fullness. "Milk-white. Milk-white for suckling."

She trembled, with liquid, mindless shivers. She felt his lips scalding her cheek. His fingers lifted her chin. "Kiss me, Marianna."

She wanted to. Badly. But some part of her wouldn't submit to being just another woman in his bed, in his life. "Go get one of the Indian women off the reservation. That's what you use them for, isn't it?"

"Is that what you think?" He jerked her up against him so that her exposed breasts were crushed painfully against the hard muscles of his chest. Pinpoints of anger flared in his eyes. "There's only been one. And at least she wasn't afraid to be a woman."

"I didn't mean it that way. That I was better."

"Then what did you mean?"

She squirmed in the steel band of his arm. She forced back her pride and gave him an honest answer. "I was jealous," she whispered, shamed.

"Don't be. I never wanted anyone like I want you."

"That doesn't change the circumstances of our situ—"

She gasped, but was unable to squelch the ripple upon ripple of pure pleasure that shuddered through her as his thumb and fingers coaxed her nipple into an aching little knot, a dusky pearl. She hated her inability to control her body's betraying responses. "Please...don't."

His mouth pressed roughly gentle kisses where her pulse thudded wildly in her throat. "Next time you'll come to me. And you'll only be saying please. Period."

She tried to fight the feeling he was generating in her, because she was terribly afraid he was right. She clung to him, her fingers clenching and unclenching on his shoulders. "The bath water..."

"It's not running," he murmured into the hollow created by her collarbone.

"We really have nothing in common—you said so yourself." But her head tipped back, giving his hot mouth full access.

He slid the robe off her shoulders, and it fell around their feet. "Does it matter?"

Eyes closed, she tried to assert her will. "Yes."

He pressed one hard, jean-clad thigh between her own. There was no mistaking that rigid arousal. "No, this is all that matters."

She started to say that *he* mattered to her, but choked back the words. She wasn't thinking rationally! She shook her head violently, her hair swaying against the knuckles of his hand at her neck.

"How can you not be driven as crazy as I am by this wanting?" His lips closed over one sensitive, swollen nipple and sucked so hard that she swayed into him. "Day and night, always that damnable wanting," he whispered against her puckered flesh.

With a will of their own, her fingers worked loose the last two buttons of his shirt and drew it out of his jeans. Her hands splayed across the hot flesh of his chest. Her face lifted in the dark, her mouth seeking the maddening pleasure of his kiss. His mouth took hers, surprising her with its gentleness, invading hers, moving over hers with a possessive desire that made her his willing prisoner.

At last he dragged his mouth away, his breath a harsh rasp. "Let me make love to you, Marianna."

"You could lose...everything," she said, trying to reach for a semblance of sanity. "Attacking a prisoner..."

"You attacked me that first time," he pointed out with a low, seductive laugh.

"If the parole board learns you seduced a female prisoner in your custody..." She tried to keep the raw desire from heating her voice. "...they'll take away the service duty program from you."

"I must be as crazy as old Red Eye when he's hopped up on the firewater. But I'm still going to make love to you. One more time."

He moved a fraction to flip the lock on her door, and she was free from his hold. But like a stupid bird transfixed by a cobra, she didn't flee. Next thing she knew, Tom was stooping to scoop her up into his arms. "After this, darlin', I swear I'll never touch you again. You'll have to come to me."

"Never," she vowed.

He carried her down the short hallway, and she could feel the shifting of his lean, muscled body. "I'll wait anyway." When he shouldered open the bathroom door, the sensually exotic scent of the bath oil rising from the steaming water enveloped them.

She blinked at the sudden light and tried to fight back her wild trembling. "You can't come in here like this . . . and do this . . . this thing to me." Her protest sounded feeble.

"Oh, yes, I can." The bathroom was barely large enough to turn around in, but he angled her body and stepped closer to the immense clawfoot tub. "I can make you want me, Marianna." He lowered her into the water, which was lukewarm by now.

She came quickly to her feet, and he pushed her back down into the oil-sheened liquid. "Look, I want you to enjoy this, but I can't wait any longer." He tugged off first one boot and then the other. "I want you too much."

This time she thought better of rising and revealing her nakedness and vulnerability in the bright light of the bathroom. She struck back with words that usually served her well. "You're crude—"

"I know." As he shucked off his jeans in haste, he jammed his foot into the side of the bathtub. "Damn!"

She should have laughed, but a fever was upon her. "What is it you do to me, Tom Malcolm? And why?"

He slid into the tub, and the water inched perilously close to the top. Those work-hardened arms and legs twined around hers. His hair-roughened chest pressed against her breasts, and his wiry curls teased her tight, hurting nipples. "Damned if I know. I only know I have to have you."

His devouring kiss dragged across her mouth, and his tongue ruthlessly pushed inside. But his trembling hand touched her carefully, tenderly, as he shifted to free one of her breasts and stroke it persuasively. "Let me enter you, darlin'.'' His ragged breath heated her mouth.

Her knee wedged upward, and his hand clamped over her thigh. "Don't fight me. Let me make it good for you.''

It was foolish of her to think he would allow her another opportunity to refuse him. His hand slid up her inner thigh, and those roughened fingers softly parted her sensitive folds to take possession of her. "Here is where I want to be, Marianna. Inside you, all of me. Feeling you so tight around me. Flaming-hot and willing.''

She couldn't control herself. His silky, growling voice painting erotic images of what he wanted to do to her made her wet and wild and wanting. His stroking fingers elicited a moan from her, made her hips twitch and arch, seeking more. Seeking *him*, his big, hard, sun-toasted body crushing hers. She clamped her teeth into his shoulder to fight back the begging words that trembled on her tongue.

His body went rigid. "You're a redheaded hellcat with angel eyes!''

Her head tilted back, soaking her hair. It floated in the water around them like a fisherman's net. From beneath the tangle of her lashes she stared up into his desire-darkened face. His eyes burned with his savage need of her. She felt powerless as his hands slipped down around her hips, his fingers cupping her buttocks, anchoring her to him.

"Let me go." Her voice was muffled against his shoulder.

"Ahhh, sweet Marianna. I only wish I could."

With those huskily murmured words, he slid inside her. She gasped, but his mouth smothered her moan. "Think of how good you're going to feel," he whispered against her lips. His hips began a rhythmic driving, stroking her, filling her, until she thought she could hold no more.

"Please..." she whimpered.

"Tell me that you want me, want this, want all of me."

Her hands slid up his neck to tunnel into his abundant hair. Her lips parted, and her tongue sought his to give him his answer in an impassioned thrust and parry.

"I love kissing you," he told her, his lips caressing hers lightly, in counterpoint to the power of his body throbbing inside her. "I love losing myself in you. Open your eyes, darlin'. Look at us. Look at how well we fit."

That was an impossibility, because a pastel haziness was clouding the back of her eyes.

"Oh, darlin'," he ground out, "I'm not going to be able to last!"

Madness! Sheer madness!

She tried to speak, but a raging force took hold of her. She wasn't sure if she screamed out or not, but his mouth closed over hers in a duplication of his complete and absolute possession of her. Streamers of fire shot through her. She arched and bucked beneath him, frenetically seeking total intimacy. Jolt after electrifying jolt convulsed her body.

She was dimly aware of his trembling fingers clutching her hips. Something powerful and violent took hold of him, and a hoarse cry burst from his lips before he fell upon her, spent and shuddering.

And then there was only the soft sound of the lapping water.

In the dark aftermath, she slid her fingers through his hair. They lay entwined on her bed, where he had carried her, both of them dripping wet. Gradually the tremors that racked her body diminished. Why had she let herself be caught up in his enslaving passion? Why hadn't she resisted more?

Surely it couldn't be love, this warm, golden feeling that eddied through her. Lying in the curve of his arm, she considered the preposterous idea. Love wasn't an overpowering sexual attraction. Love was caring, through the good times and the bad. All those phrases she had uttered when she'd taken her marriage vows with Jax. They had turned out to be meaningless, but they shouldn't be. Not when love was real.

Nevertheless, she was dismayed by this strange, almost mystical feeling that possessed her. It was a sort of gentleness, a softness that flowered after a torrential rainstorm.

She was captivated by his beautiful body, and her hands deserted his hair to stroke his chest. Her fingers found the hard buttons of his nipples nested in that dark, wiry hair. From there she sought out his smooth, taut stomach. When her fingers traced the hard line of his buttocks, he caught her wrist.

Startled, she lifted her eyes to his face. His forearm was flung across his eyes. "Do you know what you're letting yourself in for?"

The question could have been taken in several ways. She chose the prosaic. "I beg off," she whispered. It was always like that between them, she thought. A desperate, insatiable lovemaking. She ached all over. Her lips, her thighs, her breasts.

He grunted softly. "Good. Because I'm not sure I could manage for the next few minutes, anyway."

She was silent, thinking about the next time, and the next. What good would it do to demand that this be the last time? He was used to having his way, and he would have her, she knew, come hell or high water.

His arm tightened around her waist. "Don't think it."

She stirred guiltily against him. "What?"

He removed his arm and stared down at her upturned face. "Don't think about ending this. I need this, Marianna. Need it until it's over between us."

She couldn't help herself. "Is that the way it was with Colt's mother?"

His eyes left her to stare reflectively at the ceiling. Beneath her head, the muscles in his arm contracted. She thought he wasn't going to answer her.

At last he said, "We'd gone up into the Sacramentos to cut wood for the winter. Red Eye and me. Because he's Mescalero, the Indian tribal council had been allowing us to use the reservation forest for years. I met Anita there, at the council house where we applied for a firewood permit. She was soft and gentle and good, completely unlike my first wife. Vivian was sophisticated and glamorous and grasping. No, that's wrong, about her being grasping. I just couldn't give her what she wanted. All Anita Kahze asked was to be here at Mescalero. My love—we found solace in each other's arms, only once. At her instigation, believe it or not. I was lonely. I could give that, give her my time.''

She waited, breath suspended, then realized he wasn't going to say any more. A small ache at what he hadn't said filled her. ''You came to love her?''

The corners of his mouth turned down. ''I didn't ask you about your ex-husband.''

Peeved, she rose up on one elbow, the curtain of her hair swinging across her bare shoulder. ''All right, what do you want to know?''

He shook his head. ''Nothing. I don't want to know anything about you. Not anything that doesn't have to do with us. With this.'' His leg wrapped around hers, and his hand grasped her hip to draw it against him. Incredibly, he was ready for her again.

Her hand pressed against his chest. ''She, Anita, has to do with us. I need to know.''

He held her pinned against his torso. Pain shadowed his eyes. ''I couldn't come to love her. Does that answer your question?''

''What happened to her?''

He sighed heavily and fell back onto the pillow. ''She knew that. That I couldn't love her. And I suppose she knew she never could quite fit into Malcolm's world. As it was, there seemed to be animosity between my father and her. Her parents were farmers, illiterate, and stubborn about the old ways and traditions. Her father was already heavy into drinking.

"I kept hoping that somehow Anita and I could keep going as we were, friends rather than lovers, and that she'd get over her dejection. And gradually I noticed that she did seem more lighthearted, gayer."

His hand made a fist, and a muscle in his jaw tightened. "You'd think I would have seen the obvious—that she was using drugs."

"Why should you hold yourself responsible?" she asked. "Even parents don't often see the symptoms in their own children."

He turned empty eyes on her. She trembled at the awful, ghastly desolation there. "Because I'm a former addict. I got hooked on some pretty heavy stuff while I was in the hospital over in Nam. Kicking it was the hardest thing I've ever done."

"Oh, God," she whispered. That explained so much—including his almost open persecution of her. She turned her face into his forearm, pressing feverish kisses against the bunched muscle, weeping as her lips sought to heal not only the outer scars but the inner ones, as well.

"Alcohol and drugs, they're destroying the Indian," he continued in a voice devoid of emotion. "By the time I noticed Anita's condition, it was too late to do anything. She didn't want help. Wouldn't even marry me when she found out she was pregnant. I was to the point of forcibly abducting her from her parents, where I could wean her from her addiction. But she went into labor early, and Colt was born addicted. Her parents didn't want him. I got him.''

Tears streaming down her cheeks, Marianna touched his clenched jaw. "I'm sorry."

He turned his narrow-lidded gaze on her. He caught her hand in his and moved it down his flat belly. "I don't want you sorry, darlin'. I just want you in my bed when I need you."

Chapter 13

No. I'm not interested in giving out an— No, I mean it. Yes, I'm sure. Please don't call me again."

Frowning, Marianna replaced the telephone receiver. The reporter she had met in front of the supermarket had been incredibly rude when she'd turned down the interview. Something about him disturbed her.

She turned back to the telephone to dial information and asked for the phone number of the *El Paso Herald*. Then she put through a call to the newspaper. While she waited for an answer, she tried to recall the reporter's name. Jack Wilson. No, John Wilson. No. John Wheeler, that was it. The receptionist who answered assured her that no one by that name worked at the newspaper.

Marianna hung up and stood there for a moment, thoughtfully tapping her lip with her finger. John Wheeler could be a free-lance reporter—or, worse, he could be a paparazzo with one of those awful tabloids. Whatever, the man was highly suspicious. What reporter earned enough to drape his neck like a treasure chest of gold?

"You gonna pay for that call?"

Marianna turned to see Rob watching her with narrowed eyes. "I already did. I charged it to my home telephone."

Rob stared, grim exasperation tightening her mouth, then nodded. "Best get supper on early, what with it being Saturday night and all."

"Of course." Marianna's lips curled bitterly. "The trading-post hoedown." After the first time, she'd never been allowed to go back. Foolishly, she felt like Cinderella, left behind while everyone else went to the ball.

Rob's expression eased somewhat. Since the episode with the vinegaroon, she had been forced to admit to a grudging respect. True, Marianna had been scared, but she hadn't backed down or run away.

"Actually, what with the truck picking up the cattle this morning," Rob said, "we'll be going to the auction first. Everyone'll be heading out to the trading post later."

At dinner that evening the talk centered around the country fair coming up at the end of the month. "You gonna ride in the rodeo, Colt?" Tom asked.

Colt gave that mysterious half smile of his. "Gonna try."

"I'll be hitting the women's building," Emmitt rumbled, his lids blinking with each bite he took. "A man can get some real home-cooked food there."

"I notice you've been clearing your plate of every morsel of food lately," Marianna said, unable to repress a sly smile.

"Yup. A man's gotta eat."

"When I was in the 4-H Club," Rob said, "all the other girls exhibited their cooking or sewing."

Tom finished eating and settled back on the two rear legs of his chair. "Yeah." He grinned, taking out a cigar. "But you insisted on entering the horse project."

"And I won first prize, too." She glanced at Shyloh. "Wanna go to the auction tonight?"

Shyloh, her mouth full of navy beans, could only nod enthusiastically.

"Hey, Tom, how about Miss McKenna going to the trading-post dance again tonight?" Bobby asked. "Be too many folks there for that sumbitch Reese—pardon me, ma'am—to single her out."

Marianna could tell that Tom was getting ready to say no, so she said quickly, "I'd like that, Bobby."

Tom's chair came down on all four legs. His mouth clamped down on the cigar. "Just a minute—"

"Let her," Rob said, her smile a fine-edged line. "Besides, Tom, when Bobby was on the service duty program, *he* went every Saturday night. Remember?"

"You going to wear something pretty, Mom?" Shyloh asked innocently. "Wear one of those pretty dresses you don't wear anymore, all right?"

Tom's expression was brooding. Instantly Marianna rose and began collecting the emptied plates from the others. She wasn't going to allow him the chance to change his mind. "Give me half an hour and I'll be finished with the dishes."

For once, just once, she would like to get the upper hand on Tom Malcolm. This was such a small victory, but it was a victory, even so. Prince Charming he wasn't. An outlaw, a desperado, who had mended his fences...most definitely. Yes, a roguish outlaw.

Tom always had ambivalent feelings when he watched his cattle being auctioned off. He felt pride at the condition of his cattle, but also a certain sorrow at seeing cows he'd tended, calves he'd birthed, sent off to their doom. He knew every single cow, its dam and its sire. It wasn't just the cow's markings that he picked up on, but its distinct personality. Old Bossy, the black whiteface, for instance, was always the last one through the gate. She would probably wind up as dog food, and the calves would be herded onto a crowded feed lot to be fattened up for the American dinner table.

With a stoic sigh, he took a seat alongside the rest of the family in the sale ring's stands. Marianna had positioned herself between Rand and Shyloh, safely protecting herself against him. He couldn't blame her. He had to be crazy-reckless. He had visited the scary edge of his innermost emotions, his fears—and it was frightening. He'd always thought of himself as self-sufficient and independent. But now he suspected that he hadn't been fully functioning for years. Still, he sure as hell couldn't let passion rule his reasoning.

The auctioneer's voice came over the loudspeaker, reminding the ranchers of the conditions of sale. As always, the tension was palpable. A rancher's profit or loss for the year could be decided by the bidding. Two ringmen wielding whips drove the nervous cattle, flecked with manure, into the ring. With an inward grin of amusement, Tom watched as his Charolais bull trotted around the ring, ignoring the whip and looking for a way out.

Then the bidding began, and Tom observed the bidders pushing up the price per pound. The auctioneer declared the Charolais bull sold at eighty-three cents a pound. Not bad. The rest of the cattle he had brought for sale went quickly enough until the calf that Marianna had helped him birth came up for sale. He shot a sideways glance at her. She had recognized the calf, and tears were glistening in her eyes.

No, she'd never make it on a ranch.

Gallantly Rand bowed low before Shyloh and, straightening, gave her an infectious grin. "Dance, *mademoiselle*?"

She glanced up at her mother, and Marianna nodded distractedly. Shyloh was sorry that her mom hadn't worn the pretty yellow sundress that made her look like a sunflower, but she hadn't had time to change. Instead she just had on jeans and an old pink T-shirt.

The fiddler began playing a plaintive melody, and Shyloh followed Rand out into the midst of the couples crowding the wide patio. She had to stretch to put her hand in Rand's. She settled for slipping her arm around his waist instead of his shoulders. She liked him. He treated her like a grown-up. He was the best brother a sister could have. Him and Colt. She liked to draw Colt. He was different. But all her drawings of him came out looking like stick figures. It frustrated her.

"How come Colt's not dancing, too, Rand?"

The smile faded from his handsome face. He glanced over at his half brother, who was standing near a pickup. His boot propped on the bumper, Colt seemed to be viewing the dance with only mild interest.

"He's different, Shyloh."

"I know that. But so are they." She nodded at one of the Mexican couples on the floor. "Their skin is brown, too."

Rand shook his head. "Uh-uh. It's more than that. See, some folks feel that if you've got Mexican blood in you, you still could be a hidalgo, an aristocrat. Lots of Mexicans' great-grandparents were big landowners hereabouts. But Indian blood . . ." He shook his head again. "Uh-uh. Nothing aristocratic there, folks'll say."

"Does it matter? Having Indian blood in you?"

"That depends on who you are. Me? I don't give a hoot one way or the other. Colt? It's important to him. Say, why all the questions?"

"I'm just trying to understand grown-ups. Trying to figure out why they're smart."

Rand threw back his head and laughed. "I'd say you're a heck of a lot smarter than a lot of 'em, Shyloh."

She liked Rand's laugh. It came easily. But she liked Colt's smile even more, maybe because it was so rare. After the dance, rather than return to her mom, who was talking with that lady named Ruthie, she pushed through the towering adults until she reached Colt, who was still leaning indolently against the old pickup. "Would you dance with me?"

His analytical eyes surveyed the crowd, then came back to settle on her face. "I don't think that would be a good idea, Shy."

She didn't question his statement, maybe because his use of the nickname pleased her so. Instead she hoisted herself atop the old pickup fender, perching next to him. "I've been thinking, Colt. About what you said about going to college. And not having any money."

"Yes?"

"I think you ought to ride broncs in the rodeo. You'd be good. I just know it. The best. I bet you could win enough extra money to go to college somewhere, especially if you got a scholarship, too."

He smiled slowly. "You do a lot of thinking, don't you, kid?"

"I told you, I'm not a kid. Well? What do you think? About bronco-busting for money?"

He put his hands underneath her armpits and lifted her down from the fender. "I think you'd better get back to your mom, Shy, 'fore she starts worrying about you."

Who did they think they were foolin'?

Rob watched the couples sashaying around the floor, their mouths stretched with silly smiles and their eyes all glittering like a raccoon's at night. Romance? Hmmph! Their dignified ten-dollar word for nature's urge to breed, that was all it was.

Her black eyes deepened as she watched Bobby, with a stupid grin on his face, tip his turkey-feather hat to Ruthie, who in turn smiled with delight. So much for her plot to throw Bobby and that McKenna woman together. After Bobby tugged the ranch woman out onto the floor, Rob's gaze searched out the movie actress and found her talking earnestly to Red Eye. Well, Red Eye was better than Tom.

Rob jammed her hands in her pockets and sauntered inside the trading post. Edging her way past the customers lined up for beer and sodas, she sought out the pool table wedged between the last aisle and the storage room wall. There was just barely enough room around the table to circle for a shot. She called out to Emmitt, who was standing by the water cooler downing a Mexican beer. "Hey, wanna run the table with me?"

Emmitt's lids blinked at a good thirty mph. "Naw, I'm waiting on a filly to get here and dance."

Disgusted, Rob picked up a cue. When Emmitt got the birds 'n' bees in his mind, things were in a bad way. What was so great about mating? Horses were smart enough to get it over with and get back to better things. Not humans, though. No, sir, they had to moon and mope around so they could justify what horses accepted naturally.

Her nagging thoughts turned to Tom and that actress. What would she do if her brother openly courted the woman, in defiance of his own rules about prisoners mixing with the opposite sex? A sick feeling churned in Rob's stomach. Where would she go if Tom didn't need her anymore, if Marianna McKenna took her place?

I've simply got to think of something, some other way, to make the woman leave. And quick.

"Come on, Red Eye," Marianna said. "You've had too much to drink."

The old Indian held up a finger and grinned crazily. "Jush getting shtarted."

"Well, let's drink in the back of Tom's pickup," she suggested in an amiable voice. "Then you won't have to worry about finding a place to sleep."

Eyes wide with alarm, Red Eye suddenly swayed on his feet. "Dust devil?"

She had to smile. "No, *that* old devil—drink." She took his wiry arm and propelled him toward the parked cars, half staggering under his weight.

"Just a minute, gal."

She looked over her shoulder. It was Reese, and his smile looked like a death grimace. She paused to face him, mentally preparing herself for unpleasantness.

He crossed his arms, and his lead-colored eyes slid over her, making her feel dirty. "You two been to the shooting gallery or something?"

"Shooting gallery?" For a second she thought he was referring to one of the games at the county fair.

"Yeah," he said, his grin mean. "You know, shooting up. Needles. Dope."

The hair on her arms prickled. Here was danger. Real danger. "It's nothing like that," she said, hating the tremor she heard in her voice. "Red Eye has simply had a little too much to drink."

"You don't walk none too steady yourself, ma'am."

Her teeth clenched in an attempt to control her shaking. "I haven't been drinking."

He acted as if he hadn't heard her. "I guess I'll have to toss you both into the hoosegow for drunkenness."

"No, you can't do—"

But Reese already had the old man by the arm.

"Jush a shecond there, palefashe," Red Eye said, trying with exaggerated dignity to withdraw his arm from Reese's grip.

Reese drew the pistol from his holster. "Don't give me any trouble, 'cause I still hold with the theory that the only good Indian is a dead Indian."

She spun around, her gaze frantically searching the crowd. There! She spotted Tom talking to another rancher. "Tom!" she screamed out.

His head turned toward her. Something in her face must have warned him. Without another word to his companion, Tom wended his way through the press of people to reach her. "What's going on?" he demanded.

"He's trying to arrest us for drunkenness!" she said.

Tom turned to the sheriff, and his lips drew back over his teeth like those of a wolf hungry for blood. "There's nothing that says a person can't drink here."

"They're disturbing the peace," Reese countered.

"There are a hundred witnesses here who'll say you're wrong. And election time isn't that far off. Now, release the old man."

Rand and Colt sidled up to Tom's side, and Rand told Reese, "Or else my pa'll and us'll whup you—like old-time butter."

The merrymakers were drifting over to see what was happening. Reese glowered at the Malcolm men. "This isn't over yet, boys."

He shouldered his way out through the curious crowd, and Marianna felt a sigh of released tension ease out of her. Colt took Red Eye aside, leading him toward Emmitt's pickup, and Tom grabbed her arm. The smile on his face was as mean as Reese's had been. "Come on," he said, "we're going to dance. This was what you wanted, wasn't it?"

Wishing things could be different, Marianna let him draw her into his arms for the next dance. She felt Rob's spiteful gaze on her and was relieved when the woman merely asked to take Shyloh home with her. Shyloh did look tired and ready to leave.

"Why are you doing this?" Marianna asked him after the other two left. "Why are you flaunting our relationship like this?"

"Why hide it?" he muttered. He wouldn't look at her, just stared off over the heads of the other dancers. "The damage is done now. You just had to come here, didn't you? Now Reese won't stop until he shuts down Mescalero."

"It wasn't my fault."

"Shut up." His arm banded her waist tightly, and he stared down at her with angry eyes. "Do you want me, darlin'? Do you want me to kiss you? Here?"

She trembled violently as he lowered his head, his lips brushing her temple with tantalizing gentleness. But the low purr of his voice was underlaid with barely controlled rage. His recklessness frightened her. "No. Don't do this, Tom. Don't force Reese's hand."

"There's not a damn thing I'll let him do about us. You're mine to do with as I want, awarded to me by the highest authority in the district."

He fitted his jaw against her temple. His sensual power emanated like heat waves through his Western shirt and tight jeans to flow over the front of her, to seep inside her, whispering of his passion, a passion that fed on hers. Helpless against this drugging onslaught, she pressed against him. She should have been offended by his proprietary attitude, but she guessed its source. It was easier for him to say, "I want, I take for myself," than "I love, I give myself."

"I'm only yours until September," she said, as much to herself as to him. "Then I'm a free woman."

He gripped her waist more tightly. "Ah, but will you ever be free of the aching need for me? For my touch? Will you get up and walk the floor at nights with my scent haunting you, with your lips burning for mine, and your body yearning like an addict's for my hands?"

She looked up into his dark face and whispered, "No. Not for a long, long time."

He stopped then and there, still holding her, as the other couples two-stepped around them. "Damn it all, Marianna." He took a shaky breath and walked off the porch.

She followed him out into the darkness, past the crowd that had thinned out, past the other cars, to his pickup. He stood there, hands braced against the cab's roof, his head lowered. She could almost feel him tamping down his desire for her by the sheer force of his will. "I wish the hell you'd never come to Mescalero."

At the harshness in his voice, she wrapped her arms around herself in an unconsciously protective gesture. "Oh, so do I. So do I!"

"It was stupid of me to go along with the parole officer's proposal." He spun around and clutched her shoulders, then groaned and shut his eyes. She saw him breathing deeply. With a visible effort, he released his grip on her and stared down at her, seemingly indifferent. "I've never seen two more mismatched—"

"Does it matter?"

A strange look filled his eyes. "Not at the moment. Come on."

She tried to pull out of his rough grip. "Where are you taking me?"

He jerked open the pickup door and hauled her inside with him. "To bed."

The pickup lights bounced all over the pitch-black, eerie desert landscape. She sat on her side, holding on to the door handle and all the while wishing that she'd never let herself fall in love with Tom Malcolm. There were hundreds—no, thousands—of men out there who would have been eminently more suitable.

Tom could certainly claim the same. A lot of women—Ruthie, to begin with—would make better wives than she would for him and Mescalero.

But then, he didn't want another wife. He wanted sex. With her.

Fighting back her pride, she sat silent. That hard, perfect profile of Tom's could have been chiseled from granite as he stared straight ahead at the white ribbon of caliche road. In the distance, blue-white lightning forked the sky. He drove more than halfway to the ranch house before he said anything. "Are you having second thoughts? Do you still want me to make love to you?"

"I never said that!" She turned on him. "You make it so hard, Tom. Why can't you just trust me?"

In the dark his eyes were luminous, feral disks. She half expected him to bring up her drug conviction. Instead, he said, "I haven't been very tender with you, have I? I haven't courted you with sweet words or adoring glances. Not anything like the scripts you must read."

She waited, wondering where he was going with this uncharacteristic honey-smooth speech. He reached out to lift her hand from her lap and pressed it to his lips. His tongue flicked each fingertip separately.

"I just want to be gentle with you, so gentle that you cry out with wanting me. I never should have lost control like I did, there at the windmill, but, God help me, I wanted to punish you. And I wanted you. You were so soft and beautiful, and so damned off-limits. Way out of my league, lady. That's why I want to hear you say it, why I want to hear you beg me, why I want to watch you moan for me while I'm inside you."

His teeth nipped the pad of her thumb then, and she gasped. She must have surprised him, because when he released her, she raised her hand to touch the taut flesh of his cheekbone and the roughened line of his jaw. "I love you, Tom Malcolm." There, she'd said it!

He stiffened. "Don't. It won't get you paroled off Mescalero any sooner."

Her hand fell away. "Is that what you think?"

"You're an actress, aren't you?" He ran his hand through hair that needed a haircut.

"You're cruel!"

"Keep thinking that, darlin'. 'Cause you don't know reality from illusion. Reality is a body aching from work and sun and wind, glamour girl. Reality is being too poor to pay attention. Reality is settling for sex 'cause you don't want love.''

"Well, thank you for the enlightenment, big boss, but now that you've made me sexually responsive, awakened all the latent passion in my body, just what do I do for the rest of my life?"

"Oh, I'm certain you'll find some Hollywood hero to fill the bill."

Hurt and humiliation at her own folly goaded her tongue. "What I'm finding is that my ardor has suddenly cooled."

"That doesn't matter." His pickup lights flashed across the ranch house outbuildings. "You and I both know that I can rekindle it again."

"You're awfully sure of yourself."

He parked the pickup in front of her cabin. "I'm awfully sure of you."

"You bastard! If there's one thing I'm sure of, it's that you don't know the first thing about lovemaking! You're nothing more than a—a dumb macho cowboy!"

She pushed open the door and bolted from the pickup. Behind her she heard Tom's boots grinding up the distance between them. Just as she reached her door, he caught up with her. He spun her around and pressed her back against the adobe wall. "You're in an awful hurry to get us into bed, darlin'."

A burning awareness of his sheer masculinity assaulted her senses as he watched her with narrowed eyes. At either side of her, his hands, tanned and

powerful, held her prisoner. She was a prisoner in so
many ways: in her desperate desire for him; in her
growing love for him. But he didn't trust her. And she
doubted if he could ever let himself love her. She did
know that she wasn't the right woman for him. Not
the kind of woman that Red Eye said had brain and
heart and sand.

"I don't want this," she whispered. "Not—"

His head lowered, and his firm, warm lips stopped
her words with such a gentleness that she could hardly
breathe. She was trapped by the rapt spell woven by
his mouth. She clung to him as his possessive kiss
turned punishing with brutal passion. His fingers
stroked her nipples through her cotton T-shirt, discovering that they were already taut, hard, aroused
buttons, as they had been since he'd taken her into his
arms back at the dance.

He lifted his head and expelled a shaky breath.
"Damn you, Marianna! How much of this is real?
And how much is just superlative performance?"

Why had she thought he could be any different, this
man who ruthlessly demonstrated his power over her?
Her breath caught on a small sob. "Let me go."

"After this." his big hand tilted her face up to his.
His thumb traced the line of her mouth, already swollen from his bruising kiss. "I've hurt you. I don't want
that."

Abruptly he opened the door and drew her inside.
She pulled at his manacling hand, and when it didn't
give she caught hold of the doorknob. He broke her

grip with a sharp tug that nearly unbalanced her. "Stop fighting me," he growled.

She lashed out. "Then send me back."

"I would," he said wearily, "if I didn't think you'd be worse off."

She laughed hysterically. "Worse off than this?"

His eyes glittered like a predator's. With her in tow, he strode down the darkened hallway. She could feel his hot anger and knew she would be its target. He yanked her into her bedroom and snapped on the light switch. "Now. Take off your—"

"God Almighty!" he breathed.

Her eyes left his hardened mouth to follow the direction of his gaze. Her free hand smothered her gasp. Her bedroom looked as if it had been ravaged by a whirlwind. The sheets had been torn from the bed. The mattress lay half on the floor. The dresser drawers gaped open, their contents—her clothing—strewn across the room.

Now she knew what victims of housebreaking meant when they said they felt as if they had been raped.

Chapter 14

Rob!" Marianna spat.

She turned on Tom, her face twisted with fury as her fists bombarded his chest. "Your sister did this! She'd do anything to make me—"

He grasped her shoulders and shook her. "Stop it. You're hysterical. You don't know that what you're saying is true."

"I do!" she sobbed. "Ask her! She did it! And all those other times. When she tricked me into searching your desk, and the time she put that vinegaroon in between my bedsheets and—"

He grabbed her wrist. "Come on. We're going to get to the bottom of this."

The night was hot and parched, and lightning forked across the sky, momentarily illuminating the yard. The lights were on in the kitchen. Both Rob and

Shyloh, sitting at the table snacking from a bag of potato chips, looked up in surprise as the door was suddenly flung wide, scaring Phrank, who streaked into the next room.

At the sight of Marianna, Rob's relaxed features took on the same harsh expression of her brother's. She glanced at him questioningly. "Something wrong?"

"Marianna's bedroom has been turned topsy-turvy. Looks like a henhouse fight."

Marianna nodded at Shyloh, saying, "Go on to bed." Her expression must have convinced her daughter that she was serious, because she left without an argument. After she was gone, Marianna yanked free of Tom's hold and stalked over to the table. "From the moment I walked in that door you've been plotting how to get me out it again. You're jealous. Sickeningly jealous!"

Rob jumped to her feet, towering over Marianna. "I am not! I just don't want to see you make a fool of my brother. A cheap actress, a drug pusher who uses people to—"

"Rob!" Tom roared. He caught Marianna's arm and moved her away before confronting his sister. "I want the truth," he said to Rob. "Did you have anything to do with destroying Marianna's bedroom?"

Rolling thunder rattled the window as Rob's blazing eyes reluctantly released Marianna and focused on Tom. "No. But if I'd thought it would drive her away, I would have done it."

"Your sister speaks truth."

All heads turned toward the hallway door. Red Eye stood there, his grin slippery, his eyes bright and red. In his hand was a tequila bottle.

"You're still at it," Tom grunted. "How'd you get hold of the tequila?"

"Swiped it," Red Eye declared triumphantly. "From sheriff!"

Tom shoved the heavy hair off his forehead and muttered, "This is turning out to be one hell of a night."

"Read tire tracks," Red Eye suggested, waving the bottle. "Read footprints outside bunkhouse."

Exasperation flickered across Tom's face. "Not even you can do that in a pitch-black night, Red Eye."

"Nooo," the old Indian conceded merrily, "but Emmitt and me, we saw big car leaving Mescalero when we come back tonight."

"What's going on?" Rand asked, wandering up behind Red Eye.

"Get Emmitt," Tom snapped to his son. "Find out what he knows about a big car on the Mescalero premises."

Rand tipped his hat. "Yes, sir!"

Tom crossed to Red Eye and took the bottle away. "Go to bed, Red Eye."

The old man distended his lip in disgruntlement. "A little wine is good for stomach. Bible hellfire missionaries said so."

"And this'll rot it. Go on with you." He waited until the Indian ambled off, then sighed wearily and went to pour the bottle's fiery contents into the sink.

Rob glared at Marianna, then swung away to pace the floor. Outside, D.O.G. barked furiously, and everyone glanced up with expectant expressions.

All at once, Rand was back at the doorway. His face was ashen. "Grass fire!" he gasped.

Lightning crossed the sky in jagged orange streaks, so Marianna didn't see the fire at first. Then, in the returning darkness, she spotted the dancing yellowish-red strip that banded the horizon.

Tom loped past her, heading for the machine shed. "Get shovels!" he barked to Rand. "Rob, rouse Emmitt! Get him out here quick. Tell him to load a drum of water on the back of his pickup."

From out of nowhere, Colt pushed past Marianna, and Shyloh, who'd come running back into the kitchen when she'd heard Rand. "I've called Deming!" he shouted back over a suddenly rising wind.

"Find Bobby," Tom threw over his shoulder before disappearing into the darkness.

Amid the scurrying family members, Marianna knelt on one knee to face Shyloh. "Get back in the house. Stay with Red Eye. He'll take care of you. He'll know what to do if—if there's an emergency."

Shyloh's grip tightened on her mother's hand. "Where are you going?"

"With them."

Once Shyloh was safely back in the house, Marianna hurried to catch up with Tom. He was in the shed, backing out the small Ford tractor used for maintaining the ranch roads. "What can I do?"

From the height of the tractor seat, he stared down at her, and she knew he was trying to make up his mind about something. "Ever seen a prairie fire fought?"

"Only in the movies."

He rolled his eyes. "Collect all the gunnysacks. Ride out with Rob or Rand or someone."

For a moment she watched as the tractor disappeared into the darkness. Thinking of how rapidly grass fires traveled, she shivered violently despite the night's parched heat. Then she whirled to gather the gunnysacks.

As she emerged from the shed, Rob and Rand were piling shovels into the back of Rand's Jeep. Colt and Emmitt were climbing into Emmitt's battered pickup. Marianna hurried over to throw the gunnysacks into the back of the truck, alongside the fifty-gallon drum of water.

"I'm going with you!" she called to Colt. For just a second his usually dispassionate face betrayed surprise; then he swung open the door for her.

She squeezed in next to Emmitt, who was driving in the lead. The pickup bounced over the potholed road. No one spoke. From one side, headlights careened toward them, reflecting Emmitt's and Colt's grim expressions. The two vehicles slowed as they passed, and Bobby leaned out the window of the other. "I saw the fire," he yelled out. "I'll be right behind you."

He swerved his pickup around and fell in behind Rand's Jeep. The parade of headlights jounced across the landscape. Every so often a lethal bolt of lightning flashed. Through the windshield, a red glow steadily expanded on the horizon. Heat even seemed to seep into the air-conditioned cab. Gradually the glow of the prairie blaze took on the outlines of distinct flames. Then the smaller grass fires, licking no more than one or two feet high, came into view.

"Let's start here, folks," Emmitt said.

He parked near a ditch, and Colt jumped out and began passing out shovels in the thick cloud of black smoke. Rob grabbed one and headed away from the flame to begin digging a ditch.

When Marianna went to take one, Colt said politely, "No, ma'am. You couldn't shovel quickly enough." He reached for a gunnysack and passed it to her. "Wet the gunnysack. When you've beaten a spark down in one spot, move ahead to the next. The other ranching families will be along shortly to help out."

She didn't protest, just took the gunnysack, wet it and ran across the field toward the closest flames, small ones that could almost be stamped out. But the heat from the main blaze, almost a mile away, fanned her face, and her eyes stung from the acrid smoke. Near her, little patches of fire danced quickly across the tinder-dry grass, leaving charred stubble in their wake. She began beating the flames with the wet gunnysack. No sooner would one fire be tamped out than another would spring up elsewhere.

Her back and arms hurt from continually swinging the wet, heavy sack. Sweat rolled down her rib cage. A flaming cow chip went spinning in front of her, throwing off sparks like a firecracker. Sometimes she seemed to be alone. Then she would catch sight of the silhouettes of the others against the fire. The next time she looked up they would have disappeared behind the flickering flames. Rob was somewhere out there with the men. Once Marianna glanced up to see Tom outlined against the main conflagration, riding the tractor and building a firebreak.

The wind blew continually. When it changed direction, she stopped to rest, her breathing hoarse in her ears. A little while later she became aware that more people had joined the Malcolms. Ironically, the glow of the flames painted the fire fighters as serene gleaners in a field at twilight.

And still the fire raged, its crackling roar deafening in her ears.

Exhausted, she paused to stare at the silhouettes running back and forth along the fire line. "It's hopeless," she muttered.

Ruthie, who was working next to her, couldn't possibly have overheard, but perhaps she had read Marianna's despairing expression. "Deming's grass rig is on its way," she called out, then stopped to cough, having inhaled some smoke. Her face was streaked with soot. Marianna imagined that she herself probably looked like a chimney sweep.

"Yeah, but the fire truck only holds three hundred gallons!" someone yelled back.

On Marianna's other side, a ranch wife shouted, "On the way here, we passed an oil tanker drawing water from the nearest windmill."

Sometime during the night two teenage girls moved among the volunteer fire fighters, passing out coffee and water in Styrofoam cups. Wearily Marianna accepted a cup of water, noting with surprise that there were red blisters pocking the backs of her hands and arms. Someone else thrust a sandwich into her hand. She thought about these ranch people. They had come to represent to her the strength of the country she loved.

Nearby, someone was saying that five ten-person crews were fighting the 120-acre fire. Her gaze anxiously searched for Tom or his tractor. She knew that fire traveled so fast that a person on its perimeters could become suddenly encircled. Even where a firebreak had been erected, a fleeing rabbit could spread the fire to the other side.

She didn't see Tom anywhere. Then, when her gaze shifted back to her own crew, she spotted him. He was shirtless, his skin streaked with black. The flickering fire highlighted the sweat sheening his body. He accepted a cup of water from one of the teenagers and, after taking a sip, splashed the remainder over his bare chest.

He caught her staring at him, and she turned back to her work. All at once the wind shifted unexpectedly. Although the fire was a good distance off, its furnace heat swept over her and the others in the vicinity.

"Fall back!" someone cried out.

As if by magic, a sheet of wall-high flames ignited before her. She dropped her gunnysack and began running back toward the line of parked cars. Her foot caught on something—a clod of dirt, or maybe another gunnysack, she wasn't sure—and she went sprawling. She spat out the dirt clogging her mouth. Behind her she could actually feel the intense heat radiating through the back of her blouse. Frantic, others swept past her. She scrambled to her feet and started running again, but she had twisted her ankle and could only manage a hobbling gait. The greedy flames licked closer. She could feel them singeing her hair.

Then Tom was there, scooping her up against him and lunging for the nearest car. He jerked open its door and dragged her inside with him. "Down!" he yelled.

Her breath was forced from her lungs by his solid weight. Pinned flat on the spring-punctured seat, she lay still, while around them whirled a maelstrom of brilliant light and furious sound. But the only heat she felt was Tom's breath on her cheek and the desire emanating from his body, pouring over her, into her.

A moment later he lifted his weight from her. Dazed, she sat up and looked out. All around them, the grass was scorched, but amazingly, the blaze had passed over the car. "The gas tank!" she breathed in astonishment. She had expected it to explode, obliterating herself and Tom.

His voice was laden with derisive humor. "The fire was traveling too rapidly. Car gas tanks catching fire is something that happens mostly in the movies."

She didn't see anything humorous about the situation. He helped her out of the car, and she saw others emerging from the vehicles where they had taken refuge. Weakly she clung to his supporting arm. Her legs were wobbling. The fire had sapped all her strength. Even her eyeballs felt dry.

She looked down and saw that the soles of her boots were smoking. "My boots..."

"Come over here," Tom told her, then drew her along to the water drum on the back of Emmitt's pickup, where he wet down first her right, then her left, foot. She clung to the hard ridge of his shoulder for balance, feeling the solidity of him, his aura of strength and purpose. He would be a safe harbor in any storm, an anchor when all the world was falling apart.

"Tom!" Rob cried out.

At the sound of Rob's voice, both Tom and Marianna turned to see the woman striding rapidly toward them. Relief played over the strong features of her face. Only then did she seem to notice Marianna. "Well, I see you escaped, too." There was no relief in her tone.

In that moment Marianna wanted to tell the Malcolms that they could drop off the edge of the earth for all she cared, but Tom was talking. It seemed to her that he was at a great distance. "You're wiped out, Marianna. Take Emmitt's pickup and go back to the ranch."

She caught Rob's derisive expression and shook her head. "No, I—" her throat was so parched that mere speech was difficult "—I'm staying with the rest of you. I can help." She would be damned if she'd let Rob prove she was weak and unfit!

Tom shook her shoulders gently, his eyes glittering pale green in contrast to his smoke-blackened face. "Listen to me, Marianna. By dawn the Red Cross will be on the job with doughnuts and sandwiches. And the oil crews and their road-grading machinery will be arriving to help mop up the major blazes."

Rob's smile was thin. "She can always help the Red Cross pass out the doughnuts. That shouldn't be too taxing."

"Shut up, Rob. Get some rest, Marianna. You're not in any condition to help right now, anyway. With luck, we'll have the fire contained by noon."

She would have argued, but there was simply no energy left in her to do more than accept Tom's strong arms leading her over to Emmitt's pickup. Limply she slid behind the steering wheel while Tom removed the water drum. He came around to the door and reached across her to start the engine. She glanced up to thank him, but behind him she glimpsed the contempt in Rob's eyes.

Frustration was the only fuel that gave Marianna the energy she needed to drive back to the ranch house. How could she survive another month at Mescalero? Rob was making it more difficult than ever just to get through the day. And then there was Tom. He would never trust her. Living within sight and sound of him, always wanting him, yet reduced to being his only at his inclination... How long could she go on?

For another month, a voice inside her answered reprovingly. Because going back to prison, losing Shyloh, was too high a price to pay for escaping the current situation, however intolerable it might seem.

But it just wasn't the next month that would be intolerable. It was the rest of her life—being viewed as a criminal by polite society. The fact that her career might be ruined was a small thorn compared to what Shyloh would have to endure whenever mention was made of her convict mother.

So what was she going to do?

As Marianna drove into the yard, a small frown puckered her brows. A yellow Cadillac was parked there. Wouldn't that reporter ever give up? She leaned her forehead against the steering wheel and drew a deep, fortifying breath before getting out to go inside the ranch house.

She reached the screen door, but her hand froze on the handle when she heard her daughter scream. Then Marianna jerked open the door and ran inside, through the main room and the dining room to the kitchen.

What she saw chilled her blood.

John Wheeler was holding Shyloh in front of him, his arm across her small neck, one hand holding a pistol to her temple. Shyloh's lips quivered, and her eyes were wide and tear-sheened.

"I told him, Mommy," she gulped. "I told him I didn't know what he was talking about!"

Wheeler jerked his arm tighter, and Shyloh winced. "Shut your mouth, kid. All right, lady. If you wanna see your daughter walk outta here alive, you'd better tell me where the other package is."

Despite her exhaustion after all she'd been through, Marianna's brain clicked into gear, frantically trying to comprehend what was going on. "The other package? What package are you talking about?"

"Don't try lying!" he snarled. "The heroin wasn't in either your house in Mesilla or the bunkhouse here, so where is it?"

A glimmer of understanding filtered through her exhaustion. "You're the one who went through my belongings!" She saw the impatience and frustration that darkened the man's face. "I swear, there wasn't another package. Only the one in the piece of luggage I mistook for—"

He waved the pistol wildly. "There was another suitcase! Worth another million on the street! Now where is it?"

"I swear...." She was near tears, her throat choked with fear. "I don't know anything about another suitcase. The police could have confiscated it. Your contact could have picked it up. But I—"

"Look, lady, I'm tired of playing games!" He thrust the pistol muzzle against Shyloh's temple again. "I'll start with your daughter first. And you'd better believe me when I say it won't bother me to kill her. Is she worth a million dollars to you?"

"You've got to believe me, I don't know—"

His thumb cocked the trigger. It made a loud click in the silence of the kitchen.

"Mommy." The one word was no more than the wafting of an autumn leaf falling through the air, but it tore at Marianna's heart.

"Well?" Wheeler demanded.

Maybe there were such things as angels. In this case, a drunken old Indian of an angel. Red Eye suddenly lurched out of the kitchen pantry, his hands cradling his head. "Aww! A tom-tom is pounding—"

Startled, Wheeler spun around.

Equally startled, Red Eye threw out his hands.

The pistol went spinning from Wheeler's grip to clatter on the tile floor. The old Indian and Wheeler went down in a tangle of flailing arms and legs. Sheer desperation drove Marianna to scramble for the pistol, which had been kicked beneath the table. By the time she retrieved it, Wheeler was up and running.

She knelt beside Red Eye. "Are you all right?"

"One hot-damn headache!" he groaned.

"Watch Shyloh. I'm going after that man."

Surprised, the Indian blinked his red eyes. "You been drinking firewater, too? You crazy loco?"

She didn't even bother to answer, just ran out the screen door. She started Emmitt's pickup again and made a sharp U-turn in the yard. Sand sprayed the windshield. When it cleared, she could see the rooster tail of dust spewed by Wheeler's Cadillac.

She set out in pursuit. Wheeler was her ticket to freedom and the proof of her innocence. And, if she didn't stop him now, what would happen next time he came back? She sure as hell couldn't depend on the local authorities—Reese and his bunch—to help.

Sometimes, as the road dipped into the arroyos, she lost sight of even the telltale flag of dust, only to regain it when she crested the rim again. She figured that she'd already left Mescalero property, but she would worry about that infraction of the rules when the time came.

After Wheeler mistakenly turned off onto an oil-field road, she knew she had a chance. The road was a dead end, terminating at a pump jack. The drug dealer would have to come back the same way.

She backed the car into an arroyo and waited for long minutes, her heart thudding heavily with each passing second. She rolled down the window, listening, and her hand closed over the pistol lying beside her on the seat. Could she use it?

Yes, dear God, yes, a thousand times over, if it came down to defending Shyloh from scum like Wheeler!

Three minutes later the Cadillac topped the rim and descended at a furious speed. At the last second she gunned the engine and swerved in front of it. With a screeching of tires, the car veered off into the shallow gulch that paralleled the road. Before Wheeler could recover, she was out of the pickup. He was draped across the steering wheel, and she wondered if he was hurt.

Shaking wildly, she trained the pistol on him. "Get out!"

Wheeler lifted his head from the steering wheel. Blood was dripping from his lip, which appeared to be split, but otherwise he seemed only dazed. She backed up a step as he pushed open the door and got out to stand unsteadily before her. "We're going back," she said. Trembling with both anger and fear, she cocked the pistol. "All the way to El Paso. And you're driving."

It was as if the Fates had conspired against her, beginning way back in El Paso, because at that moment she looked behind Wheeler and saw Rob's pickup coming over the hill. The Dodge braked to a halt beside Emmitt's pickup, and Rob shot out of the seat. She strode angrily toward them.

"What the hell's going on here, Marianna? You know better than to leave the ranch house without permission. And taking Emmitt's pickup, to boot! Stealing it, no doubt. Who's this? Your latest lover-boy? I told that brother of mine you were no good!"

Rob, who rarely said two sentences in succession, was now ranting like all the Furies combined. She was unaware of the situation, oblivious of the pistol Marianna was holding. "You're nothing but a slut who's—"

Afraid to take her eyes off Wheeler, Marianna snapped, "For God's sake, Rob, will you—"

She was too late. The young woman had already stepped between Marianna and Wheeler. Instantly the man shoved Rob into Marianna. With a deafening explosion, the pistol went off. Rob staggered against Marianna, who instinctively caught her, lowering her to the ground. On Rob's right side, just below the rib cage, crimson slowly seeped through her blouse, obliterating the black soot stains.

Rob's low groan of pain was drowned out by the Cadillac's tires spewing sand and gravel as the drug dealer roared in reverse, trying to back the car out. Marianna glanced up. She could still give chase to the man. She could flag down a patrolman to catch him, and then she'd be home free, her innocence proved, her good name restored, and her fears for Shyloh's safety laid to rest.

Her gaze slid back to Rob, who was gasping for breath, her face contorted with pain. Hatred still glittered in her eyes.

I'd have to be a fool to stay and help her, Marianna thought wildly. She'll never believe the shooting was accidental, and worse, she'll probably report me to the authorities for everything from stealing a pickup to using a gun—if she lives.

The decision was made.

Chapter 15

Marianna dropped the coin in the slot and dialed Mescalero's number with a finger that wasn't quite steady. A nurse on duty in the emergency room had applied ointment to her face, arms and hands. Even her eyebrows and hairline were singed. She stared at the wall, wondering whether the old Indian was ever going to answer. Or was he back in the broom closet, sleeping off his hangover?

"Ohhhh." It was a low groan of discomfort that passed for hello.

"Red Eye? This is Marianna. Listen to me, Rob has been shot! We're here in Deming, at the hospital. She's in surgery now. You have to find Tom and tell him. It's very serious. Do you understand?"

"Damn fine trouble!" the old Indian wheezed in a suddenly sober voice. "I tell Tom."

Marianna replaced the receiver, bit her lip, then turned and headed back to wait.

Compared to the nurses' soft-soled shoes, her footsteps sounded abnormally loud in the hallway. She directed her steps to the small, bland waiting room, where she picked up a two-month-old magazine. Unable to concentrate, she put it down and began to pace the floor. Outside, the long-awaited rain slid down the window, making the waiting room even gloomier. Even there, the nauseating smell of antiseptic reached her.

She would have killed for a cigarette right then. The inappropriateness of the thought overwhelmed her, and she gave a little cry, burying her face in her hands.

Whatever sanctuary the waiting room normally offered to anxious friends and relatives was denied her a moment later when Sheriff Cal Reese entered. With a broad grin, he rested one hand on the pistol holstered at his hip.

"Well now, Miss McKenna, if you haven't gone and done it again. Just can't keep your nose clean, can you?"

Her legs felt as rubbery as old Red Eye's. "I don't know what you're talking about."

"About shooting someone." His tiny, glittering eyes looked triumphantly at her. "One of your guardians, to be exact."

"It was an accident! I swear!"

"Let's see, now. Just how many terms of your service duty have you violated?" He braced his weight on one leg and began to enumerate on his fat fingers.

"You left the ranch. You were carrying a firearm. Oh, and I'd love to pin consorting with the opposite sex on you. 'Course, it doesn't matter. You're never gonna see the light of day as it is."

A terrible fear rattled up her spine. Goose bumps broke out all over her, and her hair tingled against her scalp. Not even the raging prairie fire had produced such excruciating terror in her. "Please...no!" she babbled. "Oh, God, no, no, no!"

"And if Miss Malcolm here dies—" he smiled broadly "—well, you're gonna fry real nice-like, ain't you, Miss McKenna?"

The Deming jail was surprisingly up-to-date. Rather than the reinforced wire that divided most back-woods jails' visitation rooms, a glass panel separated the prisoners from their visitors. The skinny deputy sheriff on duty in the visitation room opened a barred door, and Marianna entered. She was still dressed in her jeans and T-shirt, now wrinkled and streaked with soot. She wore the same frightened yet belligerent look that Tom had first seen the moment she'd entered the warden's office five months earlier. And since that moment, Tom had known no peace.

At the sight of him, she drew in her breath sharply. Almost warily she took a seat at the counter and picked up the telephone. He did the same. "Rob?" she asked, her breath a mere whisper.

"She's going to be all right, darlin'. It was hardly more than a flesh wound."

Marianna's shoulders sagged, and her eyes closed. "Thank God!" she whispered.

"Red Eye's with her now." He hated talking on the damn telephone when Marianna was right there, within grabbing distance. The old renegade-rustler strain in him urged him to storm the place and carry her off. It would be a damned fool thing to do, of course. These weren't Red Eye's "good ol' days," that golden age of the Wild West.

Instead, he was doing something much more foolish, and all for the love of a woman. This woman. Why couldn't it have been Ruthie? But no, his blood had to run hot for a woman he could never afford, who could never be happy at Mescalero, who was as out of place here as the luminous moon among mere stars.

But this woman had taught him something—that he didn't need to control everything, that he could safely let go of his feelings with her. With her help he could come back from the hell of his fears; with her help he could become whole again, capable of loving again.

From the beginning his heart had whispered to him that Marianna was innocent, but he hadn't wanted to believe it; it had been safer to keep his feelings tamped down.

She opened her eyes, and he saw the razor edge of panic flickering wildly there.

He was aware of a vein pumping furiously in his throat and a salty taste flooding his mouth. "Marianna," he rasped, "you'll be out of here soon. I'm pledging Mescalero as collateral for the 150,000-dollar bail—and forthcoming attorney expenses. But the damn process takes hours."

Lips parted, she stared at him through the wall of glass. He suspected that she was sliding back and forth between anguish and apathy. Slowly she shook her head, her fire-red curls brushing one cheek. "No." On the telephone, her voice reached him as a whisper. "I won't let you forfeit Mescalero."

"There's not a damn thing you can do about it. Now listen to—"

She stared back, her lips a tight white line, her face empty of color but for those huge gray eyes. And even they looked empty. "No. I won't leave here, Tom. I won't let you do this. I won't let you throw away Mescalero."

He gritted his teeth against the pain. "Damn it, Marianna, Mescalero is nothing without you."

Her eyes hardened, and her voice grated as she spoke the terse, killing words. "No, you're nothing without Mescalero, cowboy. Nothing!"

She shot to her feet, spun away and almost collided with the lanky deputy sheriff who opened the door for her.

Marianna supposed this was what it must be like in the eye of a hurricane. She knew she should feel battered, but in fact she was calm.

What she had done yesterday, turning Tom away from her for good, had taken all her courage, as well as the new selflessness her love for him had given her—because she knew a part of him would die if he were surrounded by concrete, that his heroic but stubborn independence would be doomed by civilization.

He was the last cowboy, and she felt such a deep sadness because she was going to lose this man who was like a feudal lord over his range principality. He would have to turn his back on the twenty-first century and lope his horse back into the past. And she couldn't ride back with him.

Instead she was once again locked away; only an old vagrant shared the jail with her, and though she couldn't see him, she could hear his peaceful snores.

"Well, howdy, Miss McKenna."

Her gaze lifted from an old bloodstain on the cement floor to fasten on Reese's toothy grin.

"Thought you might like to know that agent friend of yours called."

She sprang for the bars, and Reese quickly stepped back. "Why didn't you let me talk to him?"

"Well, now, I don't know of no rule that says I have to let you do anything."

"Wanna bet on that, Reese?"

Both Reese and Marianna spun toward the far door. Marianna's eyes widened in astonishment. Red Eye was pushing Rob, in a wheelchair with a T-bar attachment and a bottle of intravenous solution suspended from it, through the doorway.

"Miss Malcolm, wait here," the lanky deputy was calling out behind them. "You can't go back there. You have to see the—" He caught sight of Reese and babbled, "I tried to stop her, Sheriff, but the old Indian wino just pushed—"

"Shut up, Smythe," Reese growled. He swung back around to Rob. "Now you listen to me, young woman. You Malcolms may think you don't have to obey any rules around here, but—"

"No, you listen to me, you sexist, hypocritical bigot!"

Reese's mouth dropped open, and Marianna almost laughed. Who would ever have thought . . . ?

"You're the one who is breaking the rules!" Rob continued to rage. Her face was pale, except for her cheeks, which were flushed with anger. "First, I didn't press charges, because I shot myself! I was damn stupid to let it go off like that, but not as stupid as you're gonna look if the judge finds out you booked her illegally!"

She rolled the wheelchair forward, her chin jutting aggressively, and Reese stepped back a pace. "I know exactly what I'm doing!" he blustered. "That pistol—"

"*I* was carrying that pistol. We were chasing down a drug pusher, you fool greenhorn! And that takes care of her leaving the ranch, 'cause she was with me—in my custody. No rules were violated. So you get the cussed doors open. Now!"

"I just stopped by to thank you for what you did yesterday," Marianna told Rob.

The young woman was once again confined to a hospital bed. Her face had a grayish pallor, and Mar-

ianna imagined that her unsanctioned trip to the jail
had weakened her considerably.

"It was nothing." Rob's fingers plucked at the
sheet. She didn't meet Marianna's eyes, just glanced
at Emmitt, who had brought Marianna from the
county jail to the hospital.

"It was a lot," Marianna said. "You got me out of
that—" even now that she was free, an icy horror still
seeped through her at the memory of being imprisoned "—of that jail." It had taken another full day
before the papers had been processed, but she was now
a free woman. Well, free to finish out her parole at
Mescalero, anyway.

"I didn't do that. Tom did."

Marianna's brows furrowed. "Did what? You and
Red Eye came down to the—"

"You haven't seen today's newspaper? You still
don't know, do you?"

"Know what?"

Emmitt cleared his throat. "Tom got the story from
Red Eye, then contacted the state law-enforcement
agencies. The highway patrol and drug agents and all
that. Gave 'em the description of that yeller Cadillac.
They tracked it down and arrested that man."

"He confessed to smuggling those drugs into the
country," Rob added, "and admitted that you got
mixed up in everything by mistake."

So that was why Reese had hustled her out of jail so
fast this morning. He couldn't have been more oblig-
ing, the old goat. He knew his job was on the line.
And that explained all the photographers this morn-

ing who had jostled for position to snap her leaving the jail with Emmitt.

Only now did Rob shift her gaze to meet Marianna's stunned eyes. "I'm sure that in a couple of days you'll be cleared of all charges, if what the newspaper said is true. But, Marianna, I'm so ashamed. I said and did awful things. I was afraid. Afraid that—"

Marianna put her hand around the girl's cold fingers. "I know. I know, Rob. I was afraid, too. Afraid of going back to prison. I did unkind things, too. I understand."

Rob looked up at her with glistening eyes. "Don't go. Tom needs you. So do I." She managed a weak smile. "I need you to make Mescalero... more feminine."

Marianna shook her head, her curls swishing over her shoulders. "No, you'll do just fine on your own, Rob. Mescalero will have your stamp. In your own time, you'll learn to set your own fashion, not follow mine."

Rob squeezed her hand. "Stay? Please?"

Marianna blinked back her own tears. "I can't. I'm sorry, I can't."

Tom deserved better than a celluloid wife. One who couldn't do anything worthwhile—except in bed.

Once she and Emmitt were back in the pickup, he said without looking at her, "Got sorta used to your cooking, ma'am."

"Why, Emmitt, are you telling me that you're going to miss it?"

He blinked rapidly and swallowed. "Might say that, ma'am."

Once they were out of Deming, he spoke again. "Funny how the big boss doesn't think it's odd to see you scared—but doesn't think it should work both ways."

"It's his damn macho attitude," she muttered.

"Yes, ma'am."

"Emmitt, I believe that's the most I've heard you say at one time."

"Yes, ma'am."

Marianna supposed that Shyloh was off with Emmitt, or maybe even Rand. Quickly she folded Shyloh's clothes, then gathered up the teddy bear, and the eagle feather given her by Colt, and packed them in one of the suitcases.

Next she went to her own bedroom and began to pack. She estimated that it might be a day or so before she received official word from the district court that she could leave, now that her innocence was proven, but the packing was something she had to do. It committed her to leaving. It was an irrevocable step.

Even now, she thought, I only have to close my eyes to see him: the cowboy silhouette, the hat with the crown pinched and the sides curled up, those high-heeled boots, their rowels ringing like bells, his body wrapped in shotgun chaps.

Mescalero—a seductive mixture of beauty and heartbreak.

The screen door squeaked, and she called out, "Shyloh?"

"She's at the rodeo with Emmitt and Colt."

Tom's voice! Marianna whirled around.

He filled the doorway. "Where do you think you're going?" he demanded in a harsh tone.

She couldn't meet the jewel-like glitter of his eyes. "Tom, you and I both know I don't belong here. That I'm not the kind of woman you need."

His callused hands captured her bare shoulders to chafe the smooth skin. "The hell you aren't."

She backed away, running into the edge of the bed. "You need a woman who has heart, brain and sand."

Powerful hands pressed her down on the mattress. "After the fire, I figured you had all those things. And I didn't bust my butt to get you out of jail just so you could leave me."

She felt trapped under that probing gaze. She turned her head away, but his body anchored hers beneath him. "I don't want to be in love with you. I won't be!"

"Hell, darlin'," he said, nuzzling her throat, "you don't have any choice. I've been talking to the judge. Convinced him you aren't ready to be paroled just yet."

She shoved her hands against his chest, but he didn't budge an inch. "You did what? You can't do that!"

He was big and heavy and strong, with one arm under her, holding her tightly, so she couldn't move. He slid the spaghetti straps of her sundress down over her shoulders, and one large, work-roughened hand curled around her naked breast. His mouth lingered over her lips. "Maybe not, but I would, if I could. Darlin', you've got to let me make love to you so I can forget how miserable I've been without you."

His hand slid down to her waist, then followed the curve of her hip, finding the spot where her dress bunched high against her thigh. Her body writhed helplessly as he began stroking her. Fierce, unsuspected pleasure surged through her. She gasped, then murmured, quite inanely, "It's just sex between us."

"I know," he said, but his voice was full of laughter.

"I can't brand cattle."

His thumb lazily caressed her nipple. "I know."

Her body arched against his as she took a quivering breath. "I can't climb windmills."

"I know." His voice was husky as his tongue teased her parted lips.

Liquid fire from his caressing hand exploded in her. "But I could arrange for movies to be made here."

"I know." He rose up so that he could see her face. His eyes glowed. "I reckoned that if the judge couldn't keep you here, then the movie people could. One way or another, I mean to make you a ranch wife."

Her arms slid up over his shoulders, her hands plowing through his thick hair. "For a rancher, you sure do talk a lot."

"Then I'll shut up," he said with a soft laugh that was purely male, purely triumphant. He bent his head and angled his mouth over hers. His tongue invaded, claimed, dominated. She felt her own passion roaring through her, more powerful than the prairie wildfire.

When at last he lifted his head, her sigh was a quivering thread of ecstasy. She smiled up at him. "That was good," she said lovingly. "With a capital *G*."

* * * * *

Silhouette Intimate Moments

At Dodd Memorial Hospital, Love is the Best Medicine

When temperatures are rising and pulses are racing, Dodd Memorial Hospital is the place to be. Every doctor, nurse and patient is a heart specialist, and their favorite prescription is a little romance. Next month, finish Lucy Hamilton's Dodd Memorial Hospital Trilogy with HEARTBEATS, IM #245.

Nurse Vanessa Rice thought police sergeant Clay Williams was the most annoying man she knew. Then he showed up at Dodd Memorial with a gunshot wound, and the least she could do was be friends with him—if he'd let her. But Clay was interested in something more, and Vanessa didn't want that kind of commitment. She had a career that was important to her, and there was no room in her life for any man. But Clay was determined to show her that they could have a future together—and that there are times when the patient knows best.

Silhouette Intimate Moments

COMING
NEXT MONTH

#245 HEARTBEATS—Lucy Hamilton

Policeman Clay Williams wanted more than just friendship from
Vanessa Rice. But when the drug gang he was after decided to get
him by getting her, his campaign to win her heart became a race
against time, a battle to prove they had a future together before he
lost the chance—forever.

#246 MUSTANG MAN—Lee Magner

To save her father's life, Carolyn Andrews had to find a missing
stallion, and only Jonathan Raider could help her. But the search
threatened more than their safety. Now that she'd met Jonathan,
she knew it would break her heart if they had to say goodbye.

#247 DONOVAN'S PROMISE—Dallas Schulze

Twenty years ago Donovan had promised to take care of Elizabeth
forever, but now their marriage was coming to an end. He couldn't
let that happen. Somehow he had to prove that his feelings hadn't
changed and that the promise he had made once would never be
broken.

#248 ANGEL OF MERCY—Heather Graham Pozzessere

DEA agent Brad McKenna had been shot, and he knew that only a
miracle could save him. When he regained consciousness, he
thought he'd gotten his miracle, for surely that was an angel
bending over him. But he soon discovered that Wendy Hawk was a
flesh-and-blood woman—and the feelings he had for her were very
real.

AVAILABLE THIS MONTH: